CW01095436

Sweet Music

De-ann Black

Paperback edition published 2024

Sweet Music

ISBN: 9798880260201

Sweet Music is the third book in the Scottish Loch Romance series.

Also by De-ann Black (Romance, Action/Thrillers & Children's books). See her Amazon Author page or website for further details about her books, screenplays, illustrations and artwork. www.De-annBlack.com

Action/Thrillers:
Knight in Miami.
Agency Agenda.
Love Him Forever.
Someone Worse.
Electric Shadows.
The Strife of Riley.
Shadows of Murder.

Romance:
Sweet Music
Love & Lyrics
Christmas Weddings
Fairytale Christmas on the Island
The Cure for Love at Christmas
Vintage Dress Shop on the Island
Scottish Island Fairytale Castle
Scottish Loch Summer Romance
Scottish Island Knitting Bee
Sewing & Mending Cottage
Knitting Shop by the Sea
Colouring Book Cottage
Knitting Cottage
Oops! I'm the Paparazzi, Again
The Bitch-Proof Wedding
Embroidery Cottage
The Dressmaker's Cottage
The Sewing Shop
Heather Park
The Tea Shop by the Sea
The Bookshop by the Seaside

The Sewing Bee
The Quilting Bee
Snow Bells Wedding
Snow Bells Christmas
Summer Sewing Bee
The Chocolatier's Cottage
Christmas Cake Chateau
The Beemaster's Cottage
The Sewing Bee By The Sea
The Flower Hunter's Cottage
The Christmas Knitting Bee
The Sewing Bee & Afternoon Tea
Shed In The City
The Bakery By The Seaside
The Christmas Chocolatier
The Christmas Tea Shop & Bakery
The Bitch-Proof Suit

Colouring books:
Summer Nature. Flower Nature. Summer Garden. Spring Garden. Autumn Garden. Sea Dream. Festive Christmas. Christmas Garden. Flower Bee. Wild Garden. Flower Hunter. Stargazer Space. Christmas Theme. Faerie Garden Spring. Scottish Garden Seasons. Bee Garden.

Embroidery books:
Floral Garden Embroidery Patterns
Floral Spring Embroidery Patterns
Christmas & Winter Embroidery Patterns
Floral Nature Embroidery Designs
Scottish Garden Embroidery Designs

Contents

CHAPTER ONE

'Come on in.' Etta stopped knitting the Fair Isle jumper she was working on and smiled at Sylvia and Muira arriving with their craft bags stuffed with yarn. Etta had invited members of the local village crafting bee to her cottage by the loch in the Scottish Highlands for an evening of knitting, chatting, tea and cakes.

It was one of those warm summer evenings, and the windows and front door were open to let in the fresh night air. There was barely a breeze, adding to the summery atmosphere.

The living room was homely, comfortable, with a couch, table and folding chairs set up for the knitting bee. Etta worked from home selling her knitted items, mainly online. Her stash of yarn was tidily piled up on the dresser shelves in the room beside her sewing machine and the cutting table she used for her quilting. Knitting was her mainstay, but she was a keen quilter.

Etta had the kettle filled ready for boiling. Teacups were set up on the kitchen table, and a plate was piled with jam doughnuts. The kitchen door opened out on to the back garden, and the fragrance of the flowers wafted in, along with the scent of the greenery from the loch at the front of the cottage. Set on the hillside, it was a traditional white cottage with a lovely garden, along with others dotted like sweets on the rolling hills surrounding the loch.

In her fifties, with silvery blonde hair and a neat appearance, Etta was a key member of the local village crafting bee, and liked that the ladies all shared their skills and helped each other. The crafting bee nights were held once a week in the nearby castle's function room. The castle was owned by Gaven the laird. The bee members often held extra get together craft evenings at their houses as well as attending the weekly bee nights at the castle.

Muira was similar in age to Etta, and owned the sweet shop in the village's main street nearby. The shop sold popular sweets, bought wholesale, but they made their own sweets too, including Scottish tablet, toffee, nougat and chocolates. A half–finished, lilac, lace weight cardigan was tucked in her bag and she was looking forward to working on the sleeves in likeminded company.

Her niece, Sylvia, early thirties, a pretty blonde with inquisitive green eyes, had her craft bag shrugged up on her shoulder and was carrying a tray of sweets from the shop. Variegated pink yarn peeked over the edge of the bag, and she planned to knit a pair of socks. She'd moved to the village at Christmastime to work with her aunt. Now, Sylvia couldn't imagine living anywhere lovelier than their little village, especially as she lived in her own cosy niche at the back of the sweet shop, a converted cottage, while her aunt stayed in one of the local cottages.

Sylvia put the tray down on the table in the living room. 'This is our special tablet, and...' Sylvia pulled back the paper wrapping. 'I've added pieces of our new nougat. It's made with the local beekeeper's Scottish heather honey.'

'Thank you, Sylvia,' said Etta. 'It looks delicious. You two are the first to arrive. The other ladies should be here soon. But Jessy phoned to say she's running a bit late. Apparently, there's bedlam up at the castle tonight.'

Before Etta could explain, a few other women arrived in a flurry of chatter and smiles, bringing cakes with them.

Aileen, owner of the quilt shop in the main street, went through to the kitchen to help Etta make the tea. She was an attractive woman in her thirties, and wore her dark brown hair swept up at the sides with clasps.

Penny, thirties, an expert at sewing and mending, had arrived too, along with several other ladies. They seated themselves in Etta's living room, getting ready to enjoy the knitting bee evening.

Amid the chatter, Etta and Aileen brought the tea and jam doughnuts through. The ladies helped themselves to the tasty treats and cakes everyone had contributed.

'What's the bedlam at the castle?' Sylvia said to Etta before biting into a cream meringue.

'Gaven's piano arrived earlier this evening,' Etta explained. 'He wasn't expecting it to arrive until tomorrow, though he was happy to take delivery of it. But he's got himself, and the staff, in a tizzy setting it up in the new piano bar.'

'Does the laird play the piano?' said Aileen, helping herself to a jam doughnut.

Etta shook her head. 'Nooo. He's adding it to cater for the increase in guests — musicians, writers, artists, creative types, are loving the holiday breaks at the castle and the cabins on the estate. Jessy's helping him arrange it in the piano bar.'

Jessy had worked at the castle for years. In her fifties, she was a key member of staff, and the laird relied on her to assist with the running of the castle's hotel facilities.

'A piano bar sounds romantic,' Muira said thoughtfully.

Etta nodded. 'There are so many rooms in the castle, and the lounge was previously allocated as Gaven's private room, next to the guests' main lounge and whisky bar. But he's been so busy trekking back and forth to Edinburgh on business, and everything else he has to do, that he never used it. He has his own private quarters upstairs in the turret. So he decided to make it into a piano bar. Something a wee bit special.'

Etta and the bee members relaxed with their tea, cakes and sweets, chatted about their knitting, and exchanged local gossip.

'Where did you get that lovely lilac yarn?' Etta said, admiring the lace weight cardigan Muira was knitting.

'I bought it from Elspeth's knitting shop on the island,' said Muira. The shop was situated on a beautiful island off the West Coast of Scotland.

'Elspeth stocks a wonderful selection of yarn. I buy from her shop as well,' Etta told Muira.

'This variegated pink yarn is from Elspeth's knitting shop too,' Sylvia added. 'Muira bought it to knit a hat and scarf, and I snaffled the extra balls to knit a pair of socks.'

They continued to chat and enjoy their tea.

'It's been such a busy day,' Etta said, selecting a piece of nougat. 'I've packed a few orders for jumpers and other woolly knits today and posted them away. Folk seem to be buying my Fair Isle items early, ready for the colder months. Though we're having a gorgeous summer here. It's nice just to relax and enjoy knitting and nattering on a calm summer night...

Gaven was dressed for his evening run in a snug black top and black training trousers. In his early thirties, he was over six feet tall, with dark auburn hair and a fit physique. He was single by circumstances rather than choice, and many of the women guests at the castle were inclined to take a fancy to him. As did some of the local ladies, though he hadn't found the woman for him. Not yet anyway.

But romance wasn't on his mind. Getting the piano angled properly in the new lounge was his priority. He'd been ready to go for his nightly run around the loch when the delivery van dropped off the classic baby grand piano. The two men, assisted by some of the castle's staff, set the piano in the bar. After they'd driven off, Gaven decided to move the piano so that it faced outwards into the bar. And so, with the help of Walter, a mature man, a key worker and handyman, they turned the piano carefully around on the polished wooden floor until it was angled to full advantage.

Jessy had stayed to help and stood near the doorway to view the organised chaos. 'A wee bit to the left, Gaven. That's perfect. It's right under one of the chandeliers and it shows the beautiful finish on the piano.'

Two women guests peered in. 'The laird looks very fit and strong,' one of them said, giggling.

'Look at the muscles on his arms,' the other chimed–in. 'He usually wears a suit or shirt and waistcoat. I've never seen him dressed as if he's ready to go sprinting and training.'

'Gaven's always kept himself fit,' Jessy confided to them. 'He runs around the loch most evenings when he's at home in the castle. He goes swimming in the sea at the nearby cove. And he does press–ups.'

'It shows,' the first woman remarked, and then they headed away to the dining room for dinner.

Gaven stood with his hands on his hips beside the piano and surveyed the lounge. Several tables were arranged around the room, each one with a small lamp to create an atmospheric glow, along with the overhead chandeliers. It wasn't open to guests yet, but he planned to have a special evening to launch the addition to the castle's facilities.

He'd bought an Art Deco style bar with a mirrored finish. The vintage design added to the old–fashioned feeling of the piano bar. Somewhere to relax in style, perhaps tinkle the keys or listen to someone else play a romantic tune on the baby grand.

'What do you think, Jessy?' Gaven called over to her. 'Does everything look okay?'

Walter smiled on his way out to attend to guests at reception, and Jessy went over to admire the piano.

'It looks wonderful,' said Jessy. 'The dark wood of the piano looks like glass. It reminds me of the surface of the loch late at night when everything is still.'

Gaven nodded. 'It does. We'll emphasise that for the launch night of the piano bar.'

'When are you thinking of having the opening?'

'Soon. Everything's more or less ready. Tell the ladies at the knitting bee tonight that they're invited to attend. Cocktails and canapés galore.'

'I'll tell them.' Jessy checked the time. 'I'd better skedaddle. The bee will have started.'

Gaven walked out of the lounge to the reception with her. Walter waved him over to the front desk.

'Something wrong?' said Gaven, striding over to him.

Jessy paused too, wondering what was up.

'I had the radio on,' Walter said in an urgent whisper. 'I tune in regularly to the Mullcairn show.'

Gaven nodded. He was familiar with the popular radio show in Edinburgh.

'You and the castle could get a mention on tonight's show,' Walter spluttered with excitement.

Gaven frowned. 'On the radio? Why?'

'You know Laurie, the musician that's due to book in tomorrow for a creative break here?' said Walter.

'Yes, he's booked into one of the luxury cabins,' Gaven confirmed.

'Well, he's being interviewed by Mullcairn on the show this evening. I heard it advertised.' Walter told him the time the show was due to air.

Gaven checked his watch and a slight look on panic showed on his handsome face. 'What should we do? We didn't know anything about this.'

'There's no guarantee that the castle will get a mention,' Walter added. 'But they said that Laurie is due to take a creative break in a beautiful castle in the Scottish Highlands where he hopes to find fresh inspiration to write new songs for his album.'

Jessy spoke up. 'Laurie is a popular singer and songwriter. The castle's bound to be mentioned during the interview.' She was reasonably familiar with the well–known singer. Edinburgh–based Laurie was in his early thirties, and his songs ranged from pop to ballads, catering for the mainstream market.

Gaven took a steadying breath. 'Okay, keep the radio tuned in to the show,' he told Walter. 'We'll listen to it at reception and hear what they have to say.' Then he glanced at Jessy. 'Alert Etta and the ladies at the bee night. Tell them to tune in. The bookings for the castle facilities have increased recently. We're doing great. But publicity like this is worth its weight in gold.'

Jessy grabbed her craft bag that she'd packed with her knitting, buttoned up her cardigan and assured Gaven that the ladies would listen in. 'We'll back you to the hilt. I'd better get a scoot on.' And off she went, hurrying out into the night.

The loch was only a short drive down the road from the castle. She parked near Etta's cottage and hurried in.

'Etta! Tune in to the Mullcairn show,' Jessy announced, disturbing the calm atmosphere of the knitting bee and dumping her bag down. 'The laird and the castle are probably going to get a mention.' Wisps of her usually tidy brown chignon fluttered around her face in her rush to arrive on time.

Etta's enthusiasm sparked up. Mullcairn was her favourite radio presenter. A mature man in his fifties, he had a voice as smooth as malt whisky. And a mischievous sense of humour. She cast her knitting aside and hurried over to the radio.

'I've got it tuned in to the show.' Etta switched it on. 'I listen to his show all the time. I like to listen to the radio when I'm knitting.' She mainly tuned in to one of the stations in Edinburgh, especially for Mullcairn's show. The city was a reasonable drive from the village, and she liked to hear the latest news and music.

The other ladies stopped knitting and joined in the excitement.

Jessy took a deep breath. 'The musician, the singer, Laurie, is being interviewed on the show this evening. He's booked into one of the cabins at the castle tomorrow.'

'When does the show start?' Muira said eagerly.

Jessy checked the time. 'Any minute now.' She started to hear the panic in her voice.

They tuned in to the show in time to hear the opening announcement before the advertising jingles and a couple of lively songs were played to get the listeners in the mood for an evening of entertainment.

'On the show this evening, we have a live interview with Laurie about writing new songs for his forthcoming album. He's hoping to find fresh inspiration in a beautiful castle in the wilds of Scotland.' Mullcairn sounded happy to be interviewing the successful musician.

'Did you hear that?' Aileen exclaimed. 'A live interview.'

'*For those wishing to phone–in with a question for Laurie, or for me, here is the number to call.*' Mullcairn announced the number.

Sylvia took a note of it on her phone. 'Are you going to phone–in?' Sylvia said to Etta.

Etta shook her head adamantly. 'Nooo, I've never been on the radio. I wouldn't know what to say. I'd get flustered, especially if I had to talk to Mullcairn.'

The ladies knew she had a thing for the radio presenter.

'But you could leave a message for Mullcairn that his assistant would pass on to him. Let him know you enjoy his show,' Jessy suggested.

Etta adjusted her cardigan, ruffled from head to toe. 'I suppose I could. But the phone lines are bound to be busy with fans of Laurie calling in.'

Sylvia held up the number. 'Give it a go, Etta. Imagine if Mullcairn got your message.'

Encouraged by several members, Etta grabbed her phone, put it on speaker, and called the number. 'I'll be put in a queue of hundreds,' she said to the ladies as the call connected. 'I'll be lucky to—'

'You're through to the Mullcairn show,' an assistant said, causing Etta to jolt. 'Can I have your name?'

Etta was taken off guard. 'I thought I'd be put in a queue.'

'You are. We're filtering out the fan calls from relevant questions. Can you tell me where you're calling from?'

'I'm Etta. I'm holding a knitting bee night in my cottage with several members of the bee. We live in the village where Laurie is taking a creative break at the castle.'

This perked up the assistant's interest. 'Oh, so you're a local resident?'

'I am. We've just found out from our laird, Gaven, owner of the castle, that Laurie is on Mullcairn's show tonight. I only called to—'

'We'll definitely want to include you in the live chat, Etta,' the assistant cut–in. 'But I have to advise you to watch your tongue. No bad language. This is a fun show, so you can use certain words, like knickers, sparingly, but we draw the line at bawbags.'

'Got it,' Etta assured her.

'Hold on while I tell Mullcairn about you,' the assistant said chirpily.

Etta stared wide–eyed at the ladies. 'I've got myself into a right pickle. What am I going to say?'

'Take a deep breath,' Jessy advised her. 'Just keep your comments light and airy.'

'And don't say bawbags,' Aileen reminded her, giggling.

The ladies laughed, seeing the funny side of the situation.

'I don't use words like bawbags!' Etta objected, trying not to laugh.

The assistant came back on the line. 'That's a no–no, Etta, remember.'

'Yes, I was just—' Etta tried to explain but the assistant cut–in quickly.

'I've had a word with Mullcairn, and he's delighted to have you included in tonight's chat. Are you familiar with the show?'

'Oh, yes. I love Mullcairn's show. I tune–in regularly. I like to listen while I'm knitting.'

'Great, then you'll know that he has a friendly, lively, chit–chat with guests. He wants to hear about the castle and the laird, and how this could be the ideal location by the loch for Laurie to write his new songs.'

'I'll do my utmost,' Etta promised.

'Right, you'll hear Mullcairn make his introduction, but you'll be through on the live line. Listeners will hear what you say, so good luck, Etta.'

A click, a wave of panic from Etta, and she was put through on the open line.

The lively song finished playing on the radio, and Etta clutched her phone.

My heart's racing, Etta mouthed to the ladies as she sat down beside the radio. Everyone sat around, keeping quiet, excited to be a part of the fun.

'*Tonight we're talking to Laurie about his new and exciting venture,*' Mullcairn began after the song. '*He's leaving Edinburgh behind to find inspiration for his new songs in a castle near a loch in the heart of the Scottish Highlands.*'

No reaction from Laurie. Just dead air.

Mullcairn was used to guests being nervous or unsure on the radio. He prompted the musician. '*You're up for questions, aren't you Laurie?*'

A second's hesitation sounded far too long on the radio, so Mullcairn snapped into action and filled the hesitant gap. '*We have an interesting caller this evening. Hello, Etta, are you ready to have a wee chat with Laurie and me?'*

Etta took a swig of tea from the cup Aileen thrust at her to wet her whistle, and began...

'Yes, Mullcairn, I'm ready.' Etta hoped the nervousness in her voice didn't show.

The ladies nodded encouragement and Jessy gave her the thumbs up.

Bolstered by their reaction, Etta threw herself into the interview, secretly thrilled to speak to Mullcairn.

'So, Etta, I believe you live in a cottage near the castle,' Mullcairn began.

'I do. My cottage overlooks the loch and from my front door I have a view of the castle's turrets above the forest. It's a magnificent castle, set in its own estate. Guests can stay in the castle, but Gaven, the laird, has added luxury cabins to the estate. Laurie is booked into one of those tomorrow for a creative break. They've become very popular with people like him.'

'I've been hearing about this castle from acquaintances, and it's piqued my interest. What's the castle like? Is it like a fairytale castle in the heart of the Highlands? And do you know the laird personally?'

'A fairytale castle is a perfect description. It's beautiful. I know the laird, Gaven. He's a young man, early thirties, a bit of a local heartthrob, and he takes his duty as laird very seriously. He's kind and considerate and looks after the wee village community.'

'*In what ways does he do this?*' said Mullcairn, genuinely interested.

'*I'm having a knitting bee at my cottage tonight, and the ladies are here listening in—*'

'*Good evening, ladies!*' Mullcairn called to them, igniting a reaction from them that sounded clear over the phone, and resounded back to them via the radio.

'*We have a weekly crafting bee night in the function room at the castle,*' Etta explained. '*The laird is generous in letting us use the facility and provides tea and cakes for us. And he bought us sewing machines that we keep in the castle's store for our bee nights. We were going to use our bee fund to buy them, but Gaven bought them for us. He's kind and considerate like that.*'

'*Gaven sounds like a wonderful laird,*' Mullcairn commented.

'*He is, and this is a great village, a friendly community, where everyone tries to help each other,*' Etta added.

'*It sounds like Laurie is in for a nice time,*' Mullcairn remarked. '*Are you looking forward to your stay?*' he said to Laurie, pulling him into the conversation.

'*Yes,*' Laurie said. Another lull.

Again, Mullcairn jumped in, hoping Laurie would settle down, as guests often did, and continued to warm things up by chatting to Etta.

'*What can Laurie look forward to at the castle?*' Mullcairn said to Etta.

'*Peace and quiet in the luxury cabin, especially if he's intending to write his songs. The creative breaks*

14

have become popular because of the beautiful location, wonderful food at the castle, and plenty of entertainment for those that want to join in with the party and ceilidh nights.'

'*Ah, I love a good ceilidh, Etta,*' Mullcairn enthused.

'*Gaven had a piano delivered to the castle earlier this evening. Jessy, his assistant, helped to sort it out in the new piano bar that he's adding to the castle's facilities.*'

'*A piano bar.*' Mullcairn's interest perked up even further. '*Does the laird play the piano?*'

'*No, I don't think so. But Jessy knows more than me,*' said Etta.

'*Jessy! Are you there?*' Mullcairn called to her.

Jessy jumped at the sound of her name. '*I'm here. And, no, Gaven doesn't play the piano. He bought the beautiful, baby grand piano for the guests. No one local plays, at least not as far as we know.*'

'*Sylvia plays the piano,*' Muira piped–up, taking them all by surprise. '*She's classically trained.*'

Everyone in the cottage stared at Sylvia. This was news to them.

Mullcairn laughed. '*Who was that? And who is Sylvia?*'

Muira spoke to Mullcairn. '*I'm Muira. Sylvia's aunty.*'

'*So your niece could play this baby grand piano at the castle,*' Mullcairn prompted her.

'*Definitely. She trained from the age of six until she was sixteen. She even played at a couple of theatre events, and once with an orchestra in Edinburgh,'* Muira explained.

'What does Sylvia do now? And is she there at Etta's knitting bee night?' said Mullcairn.

'I own the local sweet shop in the village main street. Sylvia is from Edinburgh. She trained in baking and confectionery. She might even become a chocolatier one day. But she moved to work with me at the sweet shop. She's come up with some great recipes for sweeties.' Muira paused. *'She's here if you want to speak to her.'*

'Hello, Sylvia,' Mullcairn said, making her feel welcome to join in the live chat.

'I'm blushing,' Sylvia confessed to Mullcairn. *'My aunty fair blows my trumpet.'*

'But can you play the piano?' Mullcairn wanted to confirm.

'I can. But I haven't played in a long time,' said Sylvia.

'Why not? What happened? Did you stop training?'

'When I was a wee girl, every Saturday morning, I went to speech and drama lessons, you'd call it elocution. Then I'd have my piano lesson. I eventually gave up on the former, and concentrated on just learning to play the piano. I loved playing, but I wasn't sure if I had enough talent to make it as a career. I'd always loved baking, especially making sweeties, so I trained in that instead. I'm happy I did.'

'But if you're classically trained, I'd imagine you'd still be able to tinkle your fingers across the keys and play a tune.'

16

'*I could. Music was part of my life for years. I'm keen to have a peek at Gaven's baby grand piano. That's what I used to play.*'

'I'm gobsmacked!' Aileen whispered to Jessy. 'I never knew Sylvia could play the piano.'

Other members whispered likewise, causing Sylvia to blush even more.

'*Can you read music? Or do you play by ear?*' Laurie's comment broke into the chat, surprising everyone.

'*I can read music,*' Sylvia confirmed. '*And I can play by ear.*'

'*Oooh! Nippy sweeties! I think you've got a challenge on your hands, Laurie,*' Mullcairn cut–in, stirring up the conversation. '*Will you be eager to play the piano at the castle? Do you think it'll help inspire your new song writing?*'

'*I'm more of a keyboard player and guitarist,*' said Laurie. '*Though I have played piano. Not a grand piano, but I'll certainly enjoy having a go when I arrive.*'

'*Okay,*' Mullcairn said with a smile in his voice. '*Time for a wee jingle, followed by one of Laurie's popular hits from his previous album.*'

The cheery jingle started on cue, and Etta and the ladies weren't sure if they were still live on air and through to Mullcairn.

'Etta,' Mullcairn said in an urgent whisper. 'Keep the conversation going. We've got a load of listeners phoning in saying they're enjoying tonight's show. We'll chat with you and the others after Laurie's song.'

'Okay,' Etta told him. Then she grabbed a knitting pattern and started to fan herself with it.

'I'll put the kettle on for a cup of tea,' Aileen whispered.

'Thanks,' Etta whispered back. 'My nerves could do with a cuppa.'

Aileen hurried through to the kitchen, followed by Penny, happy to help.

'Milk and no sugar for me,' Mullcairn's voice poured through to Etta, causing her to jolt. 'I'm sweet enough.'

Etta laughed. 'And here I was, planning a relaxing night knitting with the ladies and having tea, cakes and Sylvia's sweeties.'

'Ach! Far better to have a fun night on the radio, Etta. It'll be a night to remember.'

'Oh, yes,' Etta agreed.

'What are you making tonight at your knitting bee?' Mullcairn said to her.

'Nothing but mischief,' Etta joked with him.

Mullcairn's rich laughter filtered through to her.

Etta elaborated. 'We'd been sitting relaxing, having tea and cake. It's a warm summer evening and I've got the windows and doors of the cottage open.'

'It sounds idyllic. So, you're beside the loch,' he prompted her.

'Yes, it's a beautiful part of the countryside. There are lots of wee cottages dotted around the loch area. The main street is a few minutes walk away. And as I've said, I can see the castle turrets from my front door.'

'We've had a bit of drizzle today in Edinburgh, but it's been a nice summer.'

'The village is fortunate to be shielded by the rolling hills and the forest. The weather in the summer is lovely. We have clearly defined seasons. Burnished autumns. Snow at Christmas. Fresh springs when my garden is covered in crocus, daffodils and primroses, as are the other gardens and countryside. The summers are gorgeous, and there's swimming at the cove, but I'm more of a sitting in my garden and pottering around type.'

'Oh, I don't know about that, Etta. You sound like a live wire to me.'

Etta giggled. 'The mistake people make when they picture our wee village is that it's a calm, quiet life here. But we have lots going on.'

'Including your knitting bee and crafting at the castle.'

'Yes. I sell my knitting from the cottage. Online sales keep me going very nicely.'

'What were you knitting tonight? Or should I say, what were you planning to knit?'

'A man's Fair Isle jumper. My jumpers are popular. Even when it's the summer, customers buy them for colder nights, so I'm usually knitting ahead of the seasons.'

'I love a traditional Fair Isle. Finish that jumper, if it's my size, a broad chest, plenty of length in the arms, I'll buy it, whatever the colours. I'll be happy with it.'

'Really?'

'Yes, put my name on it. I'll have my assistant send you my details. Don't be giving me a bargain. I'm paying full price. Post it up to the studio in Edinburgh. Fair Isle is a favourite of mine.'

The ladies smiled at Etta and gave her the thumbs up that she'd made a sale to him.

CHAPTER TWO

Gaven and Walter moved through to the office behind the reception desk to continue listening to the radio as guests were chattering about the castle being featured on the Mullcairn show.

'Jessy and Etta are giving a great account of the castle, and you,' Walter said while Laurie's song played.

'Guests seem pleased that the castle is getting a mention,' Gaven remarked. 'It's created a buzz tonight.'

The castle's head chef popped into the office. 'We're all listening to the show in the kitchen.' He puffed his chest out as he added, 'Etta said that our food is wonderful.'

'It is,' Gaven confirmed. 'Oh and, the piano tuner has turned up. Could you make sure he gets a supper.'

'I'll sort that out for him right now,' the chef said, and stepped away to attend to it. Then momentarily popped back to comment with a wink. 'Local heartthrob, eh, Gaven?'

The laird smiled and shook his head.

'I never knew that Sylvia played the piano,' said Walter.

'Neither did I. I'll have to talk to her about playing for us.'

Sylvia checked Laurie's website during the song. She scrolled through the photos of him performing.

Aileen leaned over for a look. 'He's a handsome one.'

Sylvia nodded. 'I'm vaguely familiar with some of his songs, but I never quite realised he looked so...' her words trailed off.

'Sexy handsome?' Aileen nudged Sylvia.

The pictures showed Laurie performing live on stage, playing keyboards, and standing out front on the stage singing to the audiences. He had a tall, lean, broad–shouldered build, and dressed mainly in jeans and a shirt or casual top. His clean–shaven, handsome face gazed out from the website, causing Sylvia to react to him.

'He is, but he doesn't have much to say for himself,' Sylvia remarked.

'He's probably nervous being on the radio,' said Aileen.

Sylvia gazed at a close–up shot of Laurie's grey eyes, a striking feature. Soulful. His sun–lightened brown hair was well–cut, but with enough length on top to tempt her to run her fingers through. She immediately shook such thoughts away. There was surely nothing but trouble brewing from letting herself be tempted by the sexy handsome singer.

The song finished and the live chat continued.

'Laurie, tell us a bit about the songs you're planning for your new album,' said Mullcairn. *'I believe you've already recorded a few and just need two or three more songs. And we've a treat in store at the end of the show. To play us out, we're airing the lead single from the album. A first for listeners.'*

'*I've recorded several songs in the studio,*' said Laurie, sparking into a chatty mood when talking about his music. '*I'm releasing the first single, an upbeat romantic number, that I hope fans will enjoy.*'

'*Romance features heavily in a lot of your songs,*' Mullcairn remarked. '*Some of them are about love lost, poignant numbers. Are they written from the heart? Or is there special someone in your life?*'

'*A lot of songs are about love,*' Laurie explained. '*It's a subject that most people can relate to. I suppose I do write from the heart, having had my fair share of heartache, like most folks. But there's no one special in my life at the moment. It's no secret that I split up with my girlfriend during my last tour. But I'm hoping that a break away from everything, staying at one of the cabins at the castle, will help me relax and find the inspiration I need to complete the other songs for the album.*'

'*What do you think, ladies?*' Mullcairn threw the question out to Etta and the others. '*Will the fairytale castle provide Laurie with romantic inspiration?*'

Etta was the first to speak up. '*I would think so. There's fresh air, peace to write in the cabin. Countryside walks through the gardens on the estate, the forest, a meander down to the loch.*'

'*And a trip to the sweet shop,*' Mullcairn added with a smile in his voice.

'*I've plenty of tasty treats to sweeten Laurie up,*' Sylvia commented lightly.

'*Are you up for a sweetie?*' Mullcairn said to Laurie.

'*I am.*' Laurie's smooth, sexy voice poured over the airwaves, sending a shiver of excitement through Sylvia.

'*What's your speciality, Sylvia? Apart from playing the piano,*' said Mullcairn.

'*Scottish tablet. Nougat made with the local beekeeper's honey. And my chocolate robins are popular,*' said Sylvia.

Laurie sounded interested. '*Chocolate robins?*'

'*I melt a blend of chocolate and pour it into little robin–shaped moulds, and then add icing details,*' Sylvia explained.

'*I don't know about you, Laurie,*' Mullcairn remarked. '*But all this talk of sweeties has put me in the mood for some.*'

'*I'll be sure to drop by your shop, Sylvia,*' Laurie promised.

Hearing him say her name sent yet another ripple of excitement through Sylvia. She shrugged it off, telling herself it was nothing more than the thrill of being on the radio.

'*You'll have a lot to tell the laird, Jessy,*' Mullcairn said, bringing the show to a cheery conclusion before Laurie's new song was played.

'*Gaven and Walter are listening in at the castle,*' Jessy told him. '*It was Walter, one of the laird's assistants and handyman, that heard about Laurie being on your show. He told the laird and me.*'

Mullcairn was delighted. '*Hello there, Gaven. Your castle sounds wonderful. I might pop along for one of your ceilidh nights. Or a creative stay. You never know. And cheers, Walter!*'

Walter grinned at Gaven. 'I got a mention!'

Gaven smiled. 'What a show. We couldn't have asked for anything better.'

A member of staff tending to the reception called through to them. 'People are phoning up for details of the creative breaks and the party nights.'

'Great!' Gaven said, beaming with excitement. He checked the folder of events he'd planned for the guests and remarked to Walter. 'We'll probably have to add a few extra dance and party nights to our regular schedule.'

'It'll be like Christmastime party season all over again, only in the summertime,' Walter concluded.

Gaven nodded. 'That's a sensible approach.' He flicked back to the previous Christmas schedule of events. 'Yes, this would work nicely. The interest is bound to perk up due to the radio show, then it'll quieten down again. But in the meantime, let's lay on a couple of extra parties for guests and visitors — and ceilidhs.'

The closing announcement sounded over the radio, and Gaven and Walter paused to listen.

'To play us out, here is Laurie's latest single from his forthcoming album,' Mullcairn concluded. *'Thank you for coming on the show this evening, Laurie. And thanks to Etta, Jessy, Aunty Muira, and Sylvia the secret piano player. Good–night, and remember to tune in with me, Mullcairn, for the next show.'*

Laurie's song started to play, and the ladies at the bee sat listening and nodding that they liked it. It was about making a fresh start after having a broken heart, but realising that his heart had mended easily, indicating that she hadn't been the one for him.

After it finished, they all breathed a sigh of relief, clicked their phones off and felt that they were free to talk without being heard on the radio. Mullcairn's assistant had given Etta the details for his jumper.

'I'll put the kettle on,' said Etta. 'We could do with another round of tea. We've hardly got any knitting done, but what an evening!'

Others helped Etta make the tea, and the chatter and laughter resounded throughout the cottage.

While Sylvia was busy in the living room, Muira explained to a few of the ladies, including Jessy and Aileen, about her niece's piano playing.

'Sylvia's parents worked in finance in Edinburgh,' Muira began. 'They still do. They married young. Started their own business, and did well for themselves. When Sylvia was just a wee girl, they sent her to piano lessons and elocution. You heard what she said about that. Then her parents started doing even better for themselves. But as they became busier with business, their marriage drifted. They stayed together until Sylvia started secondary school. It was all amicable and they remained friends. Then they split up, and all their lives were shuffled about like a pack of cards. This included Sylvia. She'd stay with both of them on alternate weeks. Eventually, she let her piano lessons go to concentrate on her baking and sweet making.'

'Were her parents disappointed she gave up the piano?' Etta whispered.

'They were more disappointed that she didn't want to work with them in finance,' said Muira. 'But Sylvia's always been a creative type. She's loved baking and sweetie making since she was a wee girl. So she trained in that, worked for a bakery in Edinburgh, and then came to join me at the shop.'

None the wiser, Sylvia walked in, smiling and talking about her new nougat recipe, wondering if they liked it.

'I'm going to phone Gaven,' said Jessy. 'I hope he heard the whole show.'

Gaven picked up the call. 'Well done, Jessy!'

'Were you listening in?' said Jessy.

'Yes, Walter and I heard you and Etta. And Sylvia. I didn't know she could play the piano.'

'Neither did any of the ladies at the bee, until Muira spoke up,' Jessy told him.

'Is Sylvia there? Can I talk to her for a moment?'

Jessy beckoned Sylvia over and handed her the phone. 'Gaven wants a word with you.'

'Gaven. What did you think of the show?' said Sylvia.

'Wonderful. Everyone at the castle is buzzing with excitement,' Gaven told her. 'I've got the piano tuner here now. But I wanted to invite you up to the castle to give me your opinion on the piano. We're all surprised and delighted that you can play.'

'I'm glad you're having it properly tuned. You should always do that after a piano has been moved around,' said Sylvia. 'I'm excited to see the baby grand. I'd be happy to pop up in the morning.'

'Come up for breakfast.'

27

'Okay.' Sylvia accepted the invitation, and then handed the phone back to Jessy.

'Well done again, Jessy,' Gaven told her. 'I'll see you tomorrow.'

Jessy clicked her phone off. 'The laird sounds delighted. I know we were thrown in at the deep end, but it was a great night.'

A tray of tea was brought through and put down for the ladies to help themselves.

'I'm still buzzing,' said Etta. 'I got to speak to Mullcairn. Oh, my beating heart.' She giggled and then took a welcoming sip of tea.

The ladies tucked into the cakes, sweets and chatted about the show.

Etta picked up the half–finished Fair Isle jumper. 'Luckily, it's a man's large size jumper I'm knitting. The colours are classic, so I think he'll like it. He's insisting on paying full price, but I'll put a wee extra something in with it. One of my Fair Isle woolly hats, or maybe a scarf.'

'I'm sure he'll appreciate that,' said Aileen.

The conversation swung around to Laurie and when he'd be arriving at the castle.

'He's booked into one of the luxury cabins tomorrow,' Jessy told them. 'A note on the booking said he was travelling from Edinburgh and due to arrive around lunchtime.'

Sylvia breathed a sigh of relief. 'That's ideal. I'll be back at the shop by then. I don't want it to look as if I've orchestrated an encounter with him. As if I'm some sort of fan lusting after him.'

'Laurie said he'd be popping into the sweet shop,' Muira reminded her.

'That's different,' said Sylvia. 'It's up to him if he wants to come to the shop.'

'Walter mentioned that Laurie is bringing his keyboard with him and his guitars,' Jessy told them. 'But he's bound to have a go at playing the piano when he's here.'

'Do you know if Gaven has any sheet music for the piano?' Sylvia said to Jessy.

'No, I don't think so.'

'I'll rummage through my things. I've got my old sheets tucked away. I'll bring some up with me to the castle.' Sylvia had kept most of her sheet music from the past and brought it with her when she moved to the village.

'That'll be handy,' said Jessy.

The chatter continued, along with planning what they were going to be working on at their next crafting bee night at the castle.

'I'll bring my needle felting,' said Muira. 'I'm making wee birds, owls, robins.'

Sylvia smiled. 'Muira's even got me into needle felting. I'm attempting a robin, so I'll bring that with me. If he turns out half decent, I'll stick him in the shop window to promote the chocolate robins.'

'I love needle felting,' Penny told them. 'But it's finding time for all the crafts I want to do that's tricky.'

The others agreed.

'I'll be mending a vintage denim jacket,' Penny added. She ran her creative sewing and mending business from her cottage. Often she used visible mending, bright coloured patches stitched with embroidery thread, to repair pre–loved items of clothing, making them wearable again. She sold these on her website. She made the repairs a design feature of the garments, using embroidery, darning techniques, appliqué and quilting hexies as patchwork repairs.

A few of the ladies planned to work on their quilting, sewing, embroidery and knitting. And anything anyone needed a hand with, or wanted to try out a new craft, the other members were happy to help.

'I'm bringing a quilt I'm working on,' said Aileen. 'I've designed it using the new range of cotton fabrics in my shop. When it's finished, I'll display it in the front window and on my website to show the new fabrics.' She opened her craft bag and brought out sample pieces of the quilting weight cotton and handed them around. 'Take any you want.'

Muira admired the pattern on the piece she held. 'I love the rich colours. They're quite opulent.'

The other ladies agreed, sharing the pre–cut, fat quarter pieces between them.

'I feel the richness of the tones will work well for all seasons,' Aileen explained. 'There are gorgeous blues, pinks, reds and burgundy.'

Etta stood up and went over to her yarn stash. She lifted a large bag of yarn and brought it over to share with the members.

'I never got a chance to show you this earlier,' Etta explained. 'The knitting company that sends me samples of their latest yarns to try out posted this to me. It's their new colours of double knit — lots of vibrant shades, some variegated, so help yourselves if you want a ball or two to take home with you. I've tried all of them and they knit up beautifully, but I'll never use them all.'

The ladies helped themselves, planning to knit small items like egg cosies or a tea cosy.

As the evening came to a close, they helped Etta clear up the dishes, folded the chairs away and then headed out.

Etta waved them off.

Sylvia walked back along the loch towards the main street, while Muira headed in the other direction to her cottage.

The evening air was calm, and Sylvia admired the reflection of the plants around the edges of the loch. The surface looked smooth as glass, and the sense of summer filtered across the village scenery. Lights shone from the windows of the cottages, and above the hills the night sky sparkled with stars.

It was such a lovely night, she almost wished the walk was longer, but within a few minutes she was outside the sweet shop with its pretty pink and white canopy.

The front window display was filled with an assortment of glass jars brimming with sweets and chocolates. Spotlights made the barley sugar and other sweets glisten temptingly.

Digging her keys from her bag, she opened the door and stepped inside. The scent of sweets and chocolate always made her feel at home.

The shop had a modern vintage quality. An array of traditional and popular sweets lined the shelves.

Rich dark chocolates contrasted with the milk and white varieties. Creamy fudge was cut into squares or sold as bars, along with toffee and Scottish tablet.

The old–fashioned counter added to the vintage vibe.

Wandering through to the accommodation at the back of the shop, she got ready for bed. The premises, originally a pretty cottage, had been converted into the shop at the front, with the rear of the property retaining a bedroom, living room, bathroom and a small kitchen that was separate from the shop's main kitchen.

There was a back garden stretching out from the shop's kitchen. The garden was deceivingly larger than she'd anticipated when she'd moved in.

Gardening was something Sylvia was interested in, and she'd attempted to keep it tamed and tidy, while eager to learn more about what flowers to add around the edges of the lawn. A couple of trees at the bottom of the garden arched their branches over, making a little arbour where a garden seat and table were situated. In the mornings when the weather was fine, she liked to sit outside and have breakfast, or relax in the garden in the evenings.

Sylvia's bedroom window let in the night air. But before going to bed, she opened her wardrobe and lifted down a small, red, vintage suitcase where her sheet music was kept.

Clicking it open, mixed emotions entangled themselves around her, and she took a few moments to sift through her feelings.

The case hadn't been opened in a long time. Not even when she'd lifted it up with the rest of her things when she'd moved from Edinburgh. But there it was, just as she'd left it, neatly packed, all her sheet music from her past.

She lifted up a couple of sheets, remembering the songs instantly, recognising the notes, hearing the tunes drifting through her memory as if they were playing for real. The scent of the white paper. The imaginary scent of the black ink.

She decided she wouldn't feel sad about the past she'd let go of. Instead, she told herself she'd be happy that she'd be playing the piano at the castle in the morning. She loved the sweet shop. Nothing would outshine making sweets and baking. Not even the music.

Though she couldn't quell the excitement at the prospect of sitting down at the baby grand...and playing again.

She had no qualms about playing. She wasn't being over–confident. It was just a sense that she'd played for so many years, from an early age, that she knew it was a part of her.

Whether she'd play the piano tomorrow, and then rarely again, she didn't know. Just because the castle had a piano bar, it didn't mean she'd play regularly. Time would tell. And she was fine with that.

Selecting the sheet music she wanted to take with her, she sat it aside, then closed the case and put it back in the wardrobe.

Climbing into bed, she lay there gazing out at the night sky, unwinding, and rewinding her radio encounter with Laurie.

His voice resounded in her thoughts. Would he really drop by the sweet shop? Maybe. She wouldn't be holding her breath. Even if he did, what did it matter? Their worlds were so far apart that it had taken unusual circumstances, like him booking into a creative break at the castle, for their paths to cross.

She might not even meet him if he was ensconced in the cabin writing his songs. Lots of guests enjoyed the creative breaks, and she probably hadn't met many of them. So why would Laurie be any different just because she'd spoken to him on the radio?

Sighing, she pushed thoughts of the handsome musician aside and thought about the beautiful baby grand piano at the castle. She couldn't wait to play it.

Hearing a piece of classical music in her mind, a romantic sonata, she drifted off to sleep.

CHAPTER THREE

Laurie couldn't sleep. As he lay restless in bed, he kept going over the night's events — the radio interview, wishing he'd been more forthcoming instead of sounding like a fool or grumpy, unwilling to chat on the Mullcairn show. Okay, so he eventually spoke about his songs, but that was only near the end of the show.

He mentally kicked himself for not making more of the opportunity presented to him. But he'd never done well in live radio interviews.

Not that this was a valid excuse.

Then there was the issue of Sylvia. She was the wildcard thrown into the media mix. Clearly, Mullcairn hadn't orchestrated it, and was as surprised as the phone–in guests, like Etta, that Sylvia was an experienced pianist.

But that wasn't what bothered him. There was something about her that triggered his interest — her voice, soft but confident, straightforward and yet she had a truly accomplished, hidden musical talent. And she was a skilled confectioner.

He'd made another mistake before going to bed, giving in to temptation, he'd checked out the sweet shop's website. It was easy enough to find in the village's main street of shops. The sweets looked as delicious as he'd imagined they would be. There were pictures of the shop's pretty exterior, inside too, all those jars of sweets on the shelves. He was tempted to buy a selection of them.

But the strongest temptation smiled out at him from the pictures — Sylvia. She looked lovely, and had a cheerful confidence that enhanced her beautiful face. Sylvia was very attractive. No doubt about that. Silky blonde hair. Clear green eyes filled with curiosity. Eyes that he felt would be looking at him, challenging him.

He'd closed the website and tried and failed to get her out of his thoughts. Romance wasn't on his schedule. He planned to relax in the cabin. Everything he needed was provided by the castle. When he'd booked the creative break, he hadn't even checked the shops in the village's main street. The loch was mentioned on the castle's website, and it looked picturesque, as did the estate surrounding the castle. He aimed to concentrate on writing new songs to complete the album, tucked into the bubble of the castle's facilities.

Now, he'd promised to pop into the sweet shop, and felt he'd been introduced to a few of the local people. Particularly Sylvia.

The laird's piano bar sounded enticing, though he'd never played any grand piano, only an upright version. He wanted to try playing the new piano, but electronic keyboards were more his thing, and he certainly couldn't play any classical music.

Tossing and turning in the hot night, he decided to get up, shower and get ready to drive to the castle a few hours earlier than planned.

Locking up his house in Edinburgh, he put his keyboard and two guitars, one electric, one acoustic, in the back of his car. He added his already packed suitcases, and drove off just before the dawn.

Edinburgh's historic spires and architecture were silhouetted against the rising fiery pink sky. A scattering of stars that had shone brightly in the night were fading fast.

He drove away from the city, wondering if the pink sky was a warning. Not that he went by things like this, but he couldn't shrug off the sense of excitement mixed with trepidation. His creative nature picked up on the atmosphere of places and people, and he often used these aspects in his songs.

Maybe there was a song in the making from his current circumstances. A song about leaving the city behind and heading to the fairytale castle near the loch.

Morning sunlight streamed through the windows of Sylvia's bedroom as she put on a summery, light blue dress. It was a thrifty vintage buy from Penny that belted at the waist and draped to flatter her slender but shapely figure. The short sleeves and classic style made her feel suitably dressed for having breakfast at the castle and playing the piano.

She kept her makeup subtle, emphasising her lips with a soft, pink lipstick and adding a sweep of mascara. Her freshly washed and dried hair hung around her shoulders.

Stepping into a pair of comfy blue and white pumps, she tucked the sheet music in her bag, and headed out into the sunshine.

The morning already had quite a bit of heat in it, and rather than drive up, she decided to walk to the castle, to enjoy the summer's day.

Apart from Bradoch's bakery, most of the shops were still closed. Muira was due to open the sweet shop within the hour, but she hadn't arrived yet.

Walking away from the main street, she headed along the edge of the loch. Sunbeams shone off the surface, and she shaded her eyes with her hand as she looked towards the forest road beyond the loch where the castle turrets peeked above the trees.

She breathed in the fresh air. Barely a breeze disturbed the morning, and the cobalt sky indicated that another lovely warm day lay ahead.

Enjoying the scenery and the sunshine, it seemed to take no time at all to reach the forest road, and from there she could see the arched entrance to the castle. It always reminded her of something out of a storybook where she felt like she was stepping into another world of romantic adventure.

The gates were open, leading to a road through the well–kept gardens and up to the front door of the castle. It too was open in welcome.

The guests' cabins were dotted out of view amid the estate, creating hubs of privacy, while being within easy reach of the castle.

As she headed up to the front door, she saw Gaven standing in reception, and he smiled when he saw her approach.

'Sylvia, come in,' Gaven beckoned to her. He wore smart dark trousers, a white shirt, tie and waistcoat. Classic money styling. His rich auburn hair was swept back from his handsome face, and his smile reached his grey–green eyes. A genuine welcome. 'Would you like to have breakfast first, or take a peek at the piano?' he offered.

'I'm eager to see the piano. I brought some of my sheet music with me.'

'Excellent,' said Gaven, and led the way through to the piano bar. It was quiet. No one was there except the two of them. He flicked the lights on, illuminating the fairly large room with chandeliers and the lamps on the tables.

Sylvia's heart jolted when she saw the classic black piano. She walked entranced towards it, memories flooding back.

'This is the type of piano I used to play,' she said, her voice tinted with emotion.

She stopped and gazed at the masterpiece of craftsmanship, then reached out and touched the polished perfection of the closed lid.

'The piano tuner left it closed,' Gaven explained. 'He said we should keep the lid down when it wasn't in use.'

'Yes, it helps prevent dust building up inside the mechanisms,' said Sylvia. 'Did he show you how to open the lid?'

'No, but it came with a booklet and I hoped you'd be able to advise me.'

'The key lid opens easily.' She lifted it to reveal the keys. Then she stood at the side of the piano. 'There are two parts to the main lid.' She showed him how to fold one hinged part back and then lift them together. 'You can prop it open a little bit or fully.' She propped it open fully.

Gaven smiled, seeing the piano as he'd imagined it would be.

'And this part, the music desk and shelf, adjusts to support the sheet music so the pianist can read it while playing,' she explained.

She reached into her bag and put some sheet music on the stand ready for playing. Then she adjusted the height of the stool to sit down.

'I see the stool has a lid on it with a storage compartment,' she said. 'That's handy. You can keep the sheet music in there.'

'I don't want to take your precious sheets,' he said.

'You can borrow them until you buy some of your own. I can suggest suitable songs. You'll need a mix of popular and classic pieces.'

Gaven nodded, glad of every bit of advice she was offering.

Sitting down to begin playing, she paused and gazed up at the lights.

'Is the lighting okay?' said Gaven.

'The chandeliers are perfect, but that small spotlight is casting a shadow across the keys.'

'Walter and I put that up last night. The step ladder is behind the bar. I can climb up and adjust it.'

Sylvia watched as Gaven climbed up and swivelled the light. Unfortunately, he kept getting the angle wrong.

'Let me try,' she suggested. 'I know what I'm aiming for.'

'Okay, but be careful.' He stood to support her and keep her safe.

'I'll be fine,' she assured him, and reached up to adjust the light, aiming it so it didn't cast any shadows on the keys. 'There you go. That's better.'

As she climbed down, one of her shoes slipped off, causing her to giggle.

Gaven laughed. 'Right, let's get you down before you do either of us a mischief.' Reaching up, his strong arms took hold of her and lifted her down.

Her giggling caused more chaos than anything, and she found herself being swept up in the laird's arms.

The two of them were laughing when Walter's voice startled them. 'Excuse me, Gaven, but Laurie has arrived,' he announced from the doorway.

Gaven, his arms full of a giggling Sylvia, glanced round and saw Laurie standing beside Walter, clearly taken aback by the view in front of him.

Sylvia saw the tall, handsome figure from the photos staring at them. He wore jeans and a shirt. Clean and tidy, but casual in comparison to the laird's attire.

'Sorry, I didn't mean to interrupt you and Sylvia.' Laurie's tone was polite but clipped.

Sylvia jolted, hearing him say her name, obviously recognising her. How did he know?

For a moment, those pale grey eyes of his looked right at her, then he turned and walked away.

Gaven put Sylvia down gently. She adjusted her dress and felt like they'd been caught being playful, but there had been nothing untoward in their behaviour. It was just friendly shenanigans.

Walter paused, unsure what was going on, pressed his lips together to prevent laughing or commenting on what was none of his business, then followed Laurie into the castle's reception area.

'That probably looked bad,' Gaven admitted to Sylvia.

'Yes, but...' Determined not to be thrown by Laurie's miffed attitude, she sat down at the piano and started to play.

Rather than hurry after Laurie, Gaven stayed to hear her play.

As if the years had folded over into yesterday, Sylvia's fingers glided across the keys, playing a classical piece of music that Gaven recognised but couldn't name.

'This is a favourite of mine.' She continued playing, filling the room with the beautiful sound of the piano. 'I love this rhapsody. It's so romantic.'

Laurie lingered in the reception, hearing the sound of Sylvia's playing waft out from the piano bar. It resonated through him, and he felt the emotion in the tune, as if it touched his heart. Or perhaps his heart's reaction was to Sylvia. She was even lovelier in real life than in the pictures.

He shrugged away the heaviness on his shoulders. Clearly Sylvia was romantically involved with Gaven. This shouldn't have irked him, but it did.

Walter unhooked a set of keys from behind the reception desk. 'I'll show you to your cabin. We weren't expecting you until later, but it's all set for you.'

Walking outside into the bright morning sunshine, Laurie squinted over his shoulder at the castle, hearing Sylvia still playing beautifully. Then he got into his car and followed Walter's car to the cabin.

Parking outside, Laurie nodded when he saw that the cabin was set amid the trees where privacy was assured. He stepped out into the mix of sunlight and shade. Flowers and greenery provided a secluded nook that instantly appealed to him. No one else was nearby to hear him playing his keyboard and guitars.

'It's a short walk to the castle,' Walter said, opening the front door and showing him around the luxury interior. 'You've got a kitchen if you prefer to cook for yourself. We can arrange for shopping to be delivered, or you can buy what you need from the wee shops in the village's main street.'

'I'll take you up on the food delivery.'

'There's a list on the kitchen table. Tick what you want and it'll be ordered for you. The fridge and cupboards have the basics — fresh milk, tea, coffee, sugar, bread, butter, Scottish cheddar and a tin of shortbread.'

'And I suppose I can dine in the castle's restaurant.'

'Yes, all the castle's facilities are available to you. Breakfast is being served in the guests' dining room at the moment, or I can have something brought to the cabin.'

Laurie's first instinct was to refuse breakfast at the castle, then he changed his mind. 'Okay, I could do with a cooked breakfast. I'll have it in the castle. It'll let me have a look around. I'm curious to see the castle properly.'

'Would you like me to help you in with your luggage before we go?' Walter offered.

'No, I'll sort that myself after breakfast. Thank you, Walter.'

'Right, let's head back to the castle. I can recommend the chef's special this morning. Soufflé omelette, grilled tomatoes, mushrooms, beans, the works.'

'Sounds tasty.'

Glancing around at the stylish interior of the cabin, Laurie liked the airy atmosphere. Lots of light wood, white and cream decor with splashes of colour from the cushions and accessories, and windows that let in plenty of daylight. It was even more luxurious and spacious than he'd anticipated, with every convenience catered for.

He had a quick peek in the bedroom, nodded that it looked comfy, with a window offering a view of the lovely flowers and greenery, and then followed Walter back to the castle.

Walking into reception, Laurie was shown through for breakfast and seated at a table. Sylvia's playing had stopped. He wished he could've heard more of her playing, but obviously she was busy entertaining the laird.

A few guests clocked Laurie's arrival, but it was the castle's policy for guests not to encroach on well–known celebrities to allow everyone a pleasant stay, uninterrupted by having to sign autographs or pose for photos.

'I'll have the chef's special breakfast,' Laurie said when offered a menu by one of the staff.

While he waited for his order, he admired the room. The castle itself was impressive. When he'd driven up he understood why it was described as a fairytale castle. It was magnificent, far larger than he'd imagined, with turrets spiralling above the roof. The dining room where he was seated showed its historic background with floral cornices, and paintings that looked like original oils, and probably they were. But there was a lightness to it, with modern elements tastefully incorporated into the decor.

Laurie was still admiring his surroundings when Gaven escorted Sylvia into the room and seated them at a table near the window that had been set aside for them. They were so engrossed in chatter and smiles that they didn't notice him at first.

Perhaps it was the strength of his gaze, but Sylvia suddenly glanced round, as if sensing she was being watched. Or sensing Laurie.

This made Gaven notice too. 'Should I invite Laurie to join us for breakfast?' He left the decision to her.

'Yes, why not.' She smiled, thinking of several reasons that she kept to herself. Not least the fact that Laurie's unsmiling face could put a dampener on the cheery time she was having with Gaven. It was no secret that when she'd first arrived at the village, she'd found Gaven attractive. He was. But there wasn't a romantic spark between them, and so they'd remained friendly acquaintances. Nothing more.

Gaven stood up and strode over to Laurie. 'Would you like to join us for breakfast?'

'I don't want to intrude on your time together.' Laurie could hear the snippiness in his voice, and then tried to redress it. 'But if you're okay with me joining you.'

'Yes.' Gaven's offer was genuine, though he wondered why he sensed a slight resentment from Laurie. Maybe the musician just needed time to settle in and adjust to things.

'We're having the special,' Gaven said as Laurie sat down at their table.

'So am I,' Laurie told them.

As if on cue, three specials were served up.

Sylvia smiled. 'This looks delicious. It'll keep me going all day.'

'Tuck in,' Gaven said, cutting into the light omelette. 'Chef excels at soufflé omelettes.'

'Mmmm.' Sylvia nodded as she ate hers.

'Is the cabin to your liking?' Gaven said to Laurie.

'It's even better than I thought. Perfect for what I need. Nice and private. Comfortable. And Walter is arranging groceries to be delivered.'

'Do you enjoy cooking for yourself?' said Gaven.

'I'm used to it. I have a house in Edinburgh. I live on my own and cook for myself, though I often dine out,' Laurie explained. 'What about you? Do you cook?'

Gaven shook his head. 'No, I'm pampered rotten. Spoiled by chef. I can cook, but...I'm better leaving it to someone else.'

Laurie's pale grey gaze focussed on Sylvia. 'What about you, Sylvia? Apart from making sweets, do you enjoy cooking?'

There was something in his tone that stirred her senses. She wasn't sure if he was trying to get a rise out of her, or if this was just his way.

'I live in the back of the sweet shop.' She explained it was a converted cottage. 'I have my own wee kitchen and like cooking, though I'm nowhere near this level of cuisine.' She referred to the chef's special.

'Chef was full of praise for your new recipe nougat,' Gaven told her. She often made sweets for the castle's guests, and the sweet shop supplied the castle with everything from toffee to chocolates.

'I'm pleased he approved,' she said. 'The local beekeeper's honey makes it extra special.'

'The new chocolates went down a treat too,' Gaven added. 'Muira mentioned on the radio that you might become a chocolatier one day.'

'That's my plan. I love working with chocolate.'

'I must try your chocolate robins,' said Laurie.

'I'll send some up with the castle's sweet delivery,' she told him.

'If you've got a sweet tooth, do not go into Muira and Sylvia's sweetie shop,' Gaven joked with Laurie. 'Whenever I walk past the window, I end up going in and being persuaded to buy sweets I didn't even know I liked.'

'Awe, you don't take much persuasion, Gaven,' Sylvia said lightly.

'Maybe not, but be warned,' he joked again with Laurie.

'I'll take my chances.' Laurie's sexy smile caused her heart to react.

She took a sip of her tea to quell her blushes.

Walter came hurrying over to their table. 'Sorry to interrupt, Gaven, but there's a fiasco at reception.'

Gaven didn't look the least bit flustered, seemingly used to daily fiascos. He put his napkin down, excused himself, and headed away to deal with whatever it was, leaving Laurie and Sylvia facing each other across the breakfast table.

CHAPTER FOUR

Sylvia's heart fluttered, and she tried not to look directly at Laurie and continued to eat her breakfast. Sexy handsome described him perfectly. But she was determined not to make a fool of herself over a man like him. He was no doubt used to women being all of a flutter. She didn't want to put herself in that category.

He wondered what she was thinking. Did she resent that he'd crashed into her breakfast time with the laird? Or didn't she like him for whatever reason? Maybe his attitude on the radio had made her prejudge him.

Unsure, he broke the tension between them. 'I heard you playing the piano. You sounded excellent.'

'Oh, I didn't know you were listening.' She smiled and blushed slightly. 'The piano is all set. You should play it yourself after breakfast.'

He'd hoped to hear her play more, but didn't have the nerve to invite her to play for him like she'd played for the laird.

'Yes.' He forced a smile. 'Perhaps I'll do that.'

'Gaven's planning a proper opening launch for the piano bar, but I'm sure he'd be happy for you to play it beforehand.'

'I'll probably wait until the bar is officially open.'

'I'm sure there's no need. You should talk to Gaven,' she suggested.

'I will.' He doubted he would.

Finishing her breakfast, she smiled politely. 'I'd better get going. A busy day at the shop.'

'You're not staying to play the piano?'

'No, I only came up to see it and have breakfast with Gaven.' She put her napkin down. 'It was nice meeting you, Laurie. I hope you enjoy your stay at the castle.'

She stood up, smiled and walked away.

Laurie hurried after her, bypassing the ongoing fiasco at reception. A guest had forgotten to pack their sporran and needed to beg, borrow or buy a replacement for the castle's ceilidh party that evening.

Laurie headed outside the castle.

He saw Sylvia walk away along the path through the lawned gardens. A profusion of flowers bordered the immaculately–cut grass, and archways of climbing roses, clematis, wisteria and jasmine led to different routes through the estate. The scent perfumed the air.

'Don't you have a car?' he called after her.

She smiled round at him. 'It's such a lovely day, I decided to walk. I enjoy walking.'

Laurie squinted against the sunlight and watched her hurry off. Her blonde hair shone like barley sugar and her pretty blue dress matched the sky. He felt himself react to her. But then he instantly clamped down on his feelings. Sylvia and Gaven were obviously a couple. Not married if a lack of rings was any indication. Not engaged either. But still...

He sighed heavily. He wouldn't dream of causing trouble between them. Besides, he thought, looking around at the castle and estate. How could he ever compete against the laird.

50

Walking away in the opposite direction towards his cabin, he glanced again at Sylvia's retreating figure disappearing into an archway of pink roses towards the trees. And then she was gone, shaded by the forest.

Breathing in the scent of the summer's day, he couldn't shake off the feeling of their first encounter. He'd never felt like this before.

His last girlfriend, a beautiful socialite, was a slow burn relationship, meeting several times at party events and resulting in him inviting her to one of his concerts. She'd been given a backstage pass. And they'd taken things from there.

The slow burn had become a fiery relationship that lasted two years before combusting. It had always been on the cards that it wouldn't last. She was a social butterfly. He wanted to find the love of his life and settle down.

But when she'd left him for another celebrity, the media circus that followed made him feel like a complete clown.

As the months passed, that three–ring furore became last year's news. Since then, he'd concentrated on his music, culminating in him creating a new album.

But with Sylvia. Bam! The effect hit him like nothing before. No slow burn. An instant spark.

Her voice on the radio, her attitude, seeing her on the website...and then seeing her for real.

He tried to reason with himself. Perhaps it was the whole moving from Edinburgh to live in the castle's cabin issue that had tilted his senses, and he just needed time to settle here before putting his heart in jeopardy for all the wrong reasons.

Sylvia was lovely though. But his life and hers were worlds apart. Okay, so her piano and musical ability helped bridge the gap. Though something warned him that he could cause trouble for Sylvia in her settled lifestyle in the village. He didn't want to be responsible for doing that. She seemed happy and content here. He was the one out of tune with everything.

His life as a singer was as settled as it was ever going to be in his profession, but he'd managed to keep his tours and concerts to a minimum, preferring to spend time in Edinburgh writing and recording new material. Despite the gossip columnists labelling him as living a wild life, he was a homebody at heart.

Recently, he'd felt there was something missing from his life, and it had caused him to hit an inspiration impasse, unable to come up with new hit songs to finish the album. Maybe life just clashed against his creativity and he needed a break away from the city. The castle seemed like the perfect escape or escapade, whatever one fitted. So here he was.

As he neared his cabin, a message came through on his phone. He reached into the pocket of his jeans, and then frowned when he saw the sender.

The trees shielded the screen as he read the message, and he suddenly felt like the warmth of the sunshine was thrown into shade.

I heard you on the radio. Congrats on working on your new album. I've split with B. I'm back in

Edinburgh. I could come to the castle. We should talk. Julia.

He didn't want to respond, but ignoring his ex–girlfriend would risk her turning up at the castle. With reluctance, he replied.

There's nothing left to talk about. We're long done. Don't come to the castle.

After he pressed send, he wished he hadn't told her not to do something. Her reaction usually resulted in her doing the complete opposite.

Biting back his annoyance, he went into the cabin. An invitation had been put through the door. He read it. He'd been invited to the ceilidh that evening. In no mood for dancing, he cast it aside, then started to bring his luggage in from the car.

Unpacking his cases, he hung his clothes up in the wardrobe, including his kilt and sporran. The ceilidh nights had featured strongly on the itinerary when he'd made the booking, and he'd attended many a Scottish night's dancing and enjoyed it. Intending to throw himself into the full benefit of the events offered by the castle, he'd brought his kilt, and two suits with him for other dinner party occasions.

But now he felt in flux, in many ways, including his thoughts about Sylvia. Would she be at the ceilidh night? She hadn't mentioned it. Or was the event for guests only?

Laurie phoned Walter to find out.

Walter's cheery tone filtered through to him. 'Ah, you got the invitation. I know you've just arrived, but it'll be a fun night to get yer skirl on. If you're up for it. Do you need to borrow a kilt? We've always got spares on hand. Sporrans too.'

'I brought my kilt with me.'

'Handy stuff. No excuses for not coming along and giving it laldy.'

'Is eh, Sylvia invited?' he said tentatively. 'I wondered if she'd be playing the piano.'

Walter wasn't fooled by Laurie's supposed casual tone. 'It's one of the guest night parties. But Gaven extends those to the members of the crafting bee. The ladies often come along. I don't know if Sylvia will be there.'

Laurie paused, churning over his predicament with his ex–girlfriend.

'Is there something troubling you?' said Walter, sensing something was wrong. 'You can trust me to be discreet.'

Sighing heavily, Laurie told him about the message from his ex.

'Ah, so you're worried she'll turn up this evening, uninvited.'

'Yes.'

'Not the type to take no for an answer?'

'That's putting it mildly. She's used to getting her own way,' said Laurie.

'Well, we're keen to provide a hassle–free stay at the castle for our guests. Interlopers can't just waltz in and disturb things. Give me her name. If she calls to make a booking, I'll explain that we're fully booked. It's true, we are.'

Laurie gave him the details and Walter noted them.

'Leave this with me. I'll deal with it,' Walter assured him.

'Okay, thanks, Walter.'

'See you at the ceilidh. There's a buffet for dinner, but if you want lunch sent over to the cabin, I can sort that out for you.'

'I'm still fired–up on that full breakfast, so I'll skip lunch and enjoy the buffet later.'

'It'll be a fun night. The ceilidh parties always are.'

After the call, Laurie set up his keyboard in the lounge area of the cabin, along with his guitars. But he wasn't in the mood for song writing, so he decided to go for a walk around the estate, explore the territory and get some fresh air.

On her walk back from the castle, Sylvia met Etta. They stopped to chat beside the loch.

'What did you think of the new piano?' Etta was eager to know.

'It's so classy.' Sylvia then confided what had happened at the castle.

'Oooh! Caught fooling around with the laird,' Etta said, laughing.

'We were just carrying on. There was nothing else to it,' Sylvia assured her.

'But Laurie was miffed seeing you with Gaven?'

'He seemed to have a look of disapproval.'

'A wee bit jealous of the laird having you in his arms?'

Sylvia wasn't sure. 'I haven't got Laurie's measure yet. I'm not even sure he knows what he wants. But I was determined not to let it put me off playing the piano. It's beautiful.'

'Do you know when Gaven's having the official opening of the piano bar?'

'No. We were going to talk about that, but then he invited Laurie to join us for breakfast.' Sylvia explained what happened.

'We can find out tonight,' said Etta. 'You're still going to the ceilidh party, aren't you?'

'Yes, I love the dancing. Muira is going too.'

'A few of us are going, including Aileen and Penny. Jessy is working at the castle, but she'll still join in a few of the reels.' Etta looked thoughtful. 'I wonder if Laurie will turn up, kilted and keen to kick up his heels.'

Sylvia pictured him in his jeans and casual denim. 'I doubt it.'

'Well, we'll see.'

Waving, Etta walked over to her cottage with the groceries she'd bought from the main street, while Sylvia headed to the sweet shop.

Muira smiled when Sylvia walked in. 'Did you play the piano?'

'Yes, it's the same type I used to play,' Sylvia told her.

'How did it feel to be playing again? Did it all come back to you?'

'It did. It felt like yesterday.' Sylvia's eyes shone with joy. 'I was so happy that I didn't fumble the notes.'

'You always played so beautifully.'

Sylvia smiled at her aunt.

'What did Gaven think?'

'He was pleased. I showed him how to set up the piano. The basics, but he's the type who'll handle this well himself once he gets used to having the piano bar.'

Sylvia's smile faded.

'Is something wrong?'

Sighing, Sylvia explained what had happened with her and the laird, and Laurie.

'Then Walter came to get Gaven to help with a fiasco at reception, leaving me and Laurie facing each other off over breakfast.' Sylvia blushed as she told Muira the details.

'So, you've got a wee fancy for Laurie,' Muira summarised.

'No.' Sylvia sighed again. 'Okay, maybe a wee bit, but he's a looker, and he knows it. I don't want to get involved in a summer romance. That's not my style. I'm happy making my sweeties, enjoying the craft nights, and not having to add romance into the mix. It complicates everything.'

Muira understood. 'How long is Laurie staying at the cabin?'

'I'm not sure. A month maybe. Until the end of the summer. But he'll be leaving at some point and going home to Edinburgh, back to his busy life in the city. And I won't. I've no intention of going back to Edinburgh and leaving the village.'

'Well, don't wind yourself up. Enjoy the ceilidh tonight. And then it's the crafting bee at the castle the evening after that,' Muira advised her.

Sylvia gave her aunt a hug. 'Yes, I'm not going to limit my fun just because there's a handsome newcomer on the scene.'

Muira nodded firmly, and then they got on with their busy day making sweets.

Sylvia stirred the mixture to make more Scottish tablet, like a creamy fudge made with butter, sugar and condensed milk, while Muira served the customers.

Aileen came in with a small bundle of pre–cut fabric samples. 'The new sweetie design fabrics have arrived.' She'd promised to order them in for the sweet shop.

Sylvia came through to the front counter. 'These are so pretty, and such a substantial weight of cotton.'

Aileen held the samples up. 'The multi–coloured sweet pattern is printed on a white background and on a pale pink background.'

'I don't know which one I like most,' said Muira. 'We want to make aprons to wear in the shop, but this fabric is even nicer than the pictures on your website, Aileen. Now I want to make oven mitts and other kitchen accessories with it too.'

'I love it,' Sylvia agreed. 'I'd even like to use this to make a quilt for my bed. Sleeping under a sweetie quilt. Oh the dreams I'd have.' She giggled.

'I ordered in two rolls of the white background and two of the pink,' Aileen told them. 'Customers have already been placing orders online, but you get first dibs. Would you like enough to make your aprons, and enough for a few accessories?'

Sylvia and Muira nodded, and then ordered extra as well.

'We'll have both backgrounds,' said Sylvia. 'But I'll need extra pink to make a quilt. You'll know better than me, Aileen, how much I'll need to make a nice quilt.'

'I'll cut what you need,' said Aileen. 'And I can suggest a quilt pattern for you. The pattern is non–directional, so that'll make it easier to work with as the print can be cut all ways.'

'Thanks,' said Sylvia. 'I'll pop over to the quilt shop later and settle up with you.'

'Would you like me to make the aprons for you?' Aileen offered.

Sylvia and Muira exchanged a glance and nodded. They could sew, but Aileen was an expert at quilting and making other garments.

'Are you sure you're not too busy?' said Muira.

'I could run up a couple of aprons each for you if you don't mind me taking photos of them to advertise the new fabrics on my website. I was planning on making something to promote the fabric, and the aprons would be ideal,' Aileen explained.

'That would be handy,' Muira agreed.

Aileen folded the fabric samples. 'Give me one of your aprons and I'll use it for sizing the pattern.'

They were both wearing white bib aprons with a front pocket styling.

Sylvia unhooked a clean apron from the kitchen, folded it and handed it to Aileen.

'I'll make a start on these today,' said Aileen, planning to run them up on the sewing machine at her quilt shop. 'I enjoy sewing things like this.' Then she added, 'Are you both going to the ceilidh tonight?'

'Yes, we'll be there,' Sylvia told her.

'Great, see you later.' Taking the apron and fabric samples with her, Aileen hurried away as customers came into the sweet shop.

Sylvia went back through to the kitchen to continue making the tablet, while Muira dealt with the customers.

A short time later, a man peered in the front window.

'Sylvia!' Muira called through to the kitchen. 'The laird is peering in the window at the sweeties.'

Wiping sugar from her hands, Sylvia went through to the front of the shop.

Gaven walked in, all smiles. 'Don't tempt me too much,' he said jokingly.

'What can we get for you today?' said Muira. 'There's the soor plooms you liked the last time or cola cubes.'

'And chocolates,' Sylvia added, gesturing to them on a carousel display.

It was then that Gaven noticed a tray of temptation on the counter.

He gasped. 'Are those frying pans?'

'Yes,' said Muira. 'Sylvia made them. They've been selling well.'

Gaven lifted up one of the little, round, tin foil trays filled with toffee. It had a lolly stick set in the toffee as the makeshift frying pan handle. 'I haven't had one of these since I was a wee boy.'

'They're a nice taste of nostalgia,' said Sylvia.

'I'll have a couple.' He popped them in the paper bag Muira held up. Then added some more.

Sylvia smiled. 'Can we tempt you with anything else?'

'I only came in to ask you something,' he told Sylvia. 'I was over at Oliver's art shop picking up paintings for the piano bar. Classy paintings that'll suit the bar styling.'

Oliver's art shop was across the main street from the sweet shop, and he was another young man who'd made a success of opening a shop in the village. And now he was working on the artwork for a picture book too.

Gaven had put the paintings in his car and popped over to have a word with Sylvia.

'What did you want to ask me?' said Sylvia.

'At the opening of the piano bar, which will be soon, would you play the piano for us?'

'I'd be happy to play for you,' Sylvia agreed.

'You'll be paid for your time,' Gaven added.

Sylvia went to object, as playing was a pleasure and it would be a fun evening, but Gaven insisted.

'Okay, what would you like me to play?' she said.

Gaven held his hands up. 'I'm leaving that up to you. I trust you'll know what songs people will enjoy and that will suit being played on the baby grand.'

Sylvia was excited at the chance to do this. 'I'll prepare a selection.'

'Are you coming up to the ceilidh tonight?' he said.

'Yes, a few of the crafting bee ladies will be there,' Sylvia confirmed.

'You're welcome to practise on the piano,' he offered.

Sylvia needed no encouragement. 'I'll bring my sheet music and try out some of the songs.'

Gaven seemed relieved and delighted.

He finally left the shop with far more sweets than he'd intended on buying. And Sylvia had given him a bag with a couple of chocolate robins for Laurie.

Walking back to where he'd parked his car outside the art shop, Gaven dug into one of the paper bags for a toffee frying pan. The taste of nostalgia was particularly sweet and delicious.

CHAPTER FIVE

Laurie walked through the verdant nooks of the castle's estate, feeling like parts of it were the perfect backdrop for a fairytale film. Sunlight flickered through the branches of the trees where pathways meandered towards areas of interest, including a wishing well, and flower gardens featuring different plants, each one with its own characteristic theme.

Deeper in the forest, the thick evergreens shielded out the brightest rays of the sun, and the ground was carpeted with lush moss and gnarled roots that looked like they were a hundred years old.

In contrast, through a wrought iron archway entwined with vines, a natural open–air pool presented itself. Laurie sat down at the edge and trailed his hands through the cool, clear water, tempted to go for a swim. But maybe another time, he thought, and got up and continued to explore the area.

The feeling of freedom and relaxation walking through the estate refreshed his senses. For a man who'd had snatched sleep the previous night, his energy wasn't waning.

During a tea break in the sweet shop, Sylvia checked out sheet music for sale online.

'I told Gaven that I'd advise him on sheet music to buy for the piano bar,' she said to Muira.

'Is there anything listed that would suit him?' Muira peered at the laptop.

Sylvia pointed to the screen. 'There's a bargain bundle on sale here. The selection of music is perfect, so many different songs to suit all tastes. Classical pieces, old–time favourites and modern songs. It's being sold for a song. Pardon the pun.'

'Buying a bundle would save having to pick individual songs,' said Muira.

Sylvia focussed on the screen. 'It's a real bargain. Someone will snap it up.'

'What do you want to do?'

'Buy it for Gaven.'

Muira nodded.

Sylvia started to make the transaction online. 'He's paying me far too much to play the piano at the opening night. I'd have done it for nothing. So this makes me feel like I've helped. Gaven's always helping other folk in the village.'

'That's true,' Muira agreed.

'There, that's it bought,' Sylvia announced with a note of triumph. 'It's a next day delivery.'

Delighted to have secured the sheet music, Sylvia finished drinking her tea and then they continued their work in the sweet shop.

Walter helped Gaven hang the new paintings in the piano bar. The three watercolours had an illustrative quality depicting a classic black grand piano on a white background, an Art Deco style couple dancing, and a decorative cocktail glass. The paintings were framed and hung on the walls of the lounge, adding to the decor.

'Oliver has made a great job of these,' Gaven commented, standing back to admire the paintings. He'd commissioned Oliver to paint them after ordering the piano. Working from his art shop in the main street, Oliver had been happy to create them, suggesting an illustrative effect.

'They're lovely paintings,' Walter agreed, putting his hammer back in his tool bag.

Talking about when to have the piano bar's opening launch night, they went through to the reception.

Jessy was dealing with guests, so when a call came through, Gaven picked it up while Walter tucked his tool bag away under the reception desk.

'No, I'm sorry,' Gaven told the caller. 'We're fully booked.'

The woman was reluctant to accept this, and it quickly became evident to Walter that it was Laurie's ex–girlfriend being snippy with the laird.

Walter waved his arms in mild panic, trying to warn Gaven. He'd briefly mentioned to him about the situation while they were hanging the paintings.

For a moment, Gaven frowned at Walter.

That's Julia! Walter mouthed to him.

Gaven nodded to Walter as the woman continued to complain.

'I heard about the castle on the radio,' Julia told Gaven firmly. 'You must have a room available for me this evening. I'm Laurie's close friend, very close, if you know what I mean, and I want to surprise him tonight.'

'As I said, we're fully booked,' Gaven reiterated politely.

'That's totally unacceptable,' she snapped at him, unaware he was the laird. 'It's a huge castle. Surely there's one room I can have. Or bump another guest elsewhere and give me their room. I promised Laurie I'd be at the castle tonight.'

'I thought you wanted to surprise him,' Gaven corrected her.

'Put me through to whoever is in charge,' she demanded, sounding annoyed that he'd picked up on her ruse.

'One moment.' Gaven clicked the call to private so he could speak to Walter. 'She wants to talk to whoever is in charge.' He gave Walter a knowing look.

'Give me the phone,' said Walter, prepared to deal with the awkward call.

Gaven handed it to him, assured that Walter's years of experience would kick in. Although the laird was prepared to handle it himself, he knew Walter had a way of dealing with situations like this.

'Hello,' Walter began. 'I believe you're looking for accommodation, but we're full to the brim.'

The uppity voice railed at him. 'That's not acceptable. I need a room.'

'No, rooms, available,' Walter clarified in a calm tone, hoping this would be sufficient.

But Julia wasn't happy. 'Is there another hotel nearby?'

'No, I'm afraid not. The castle is the wee village's main accommodation. This is a busy time of the year.

And folk phoned last night after hearing the castle mentioned on the radio and snapped up all the remaining rooms and the luxury cabins.'

But she still wanted to force him to find her somewhere.

Walter replied cheerily. 'Well, if you have a sleeping bag, you could bring it with you and ask one of the farmers to let you stay overnight in their barn.'

The mere suggestion set off fireworks in her. 'I wouldn't dream of using a sleeping bag!' she shouted indignantly.

'Ah, you're one of those hardy lassies,' Walter toyed with her. 'Throw a blanket on the ground and just rough it.'

Gaven tried not to laugh. No one could wind someone up quite like Walter.

She gasped and snapped at Walter. 'You can keep your stupid castle! I never want to stay there!' She clicked the call to a defiant close.

'Julia's not coming here after all,' Walter told Gaven.

They smiled and breathed a sigh of relief.

Jessy heard snippets of the call and frowned at them.

'I'll explain later,' Walter said to Jessy. 'We need to get things ready for the ceilidh.'

'Thanks for handling that, Walter,' Gaven said with a wink, and then headed through to the kitchen to discuss the buffet for the ceilidh with the head chef.

Laurie circled back to his cabin.

Everything about the beautiful castle and countryside resonated well with him. The vibrant blue sky, unmistakably Scottish in tone, stretched above him in a clearing of greenery where a mild breeze was all that disturbed the grass and fronds at the edge of a fairytale brook. Even the gentle flow of the water trickling over the bed of stones had turned its volume down to a considerate whisper.

For the first time in a while, he heard the hint of a melody filtering through his mind.

A few notes at first, repeating in a rhythm that felt like a chorus rather than a verse, as if the song began mid–stream, before starting to reveal the opening verse.

No words, just the music, a song so different from his recent work that he feared it would disappear like the brightness of the day was due to do.

Taking out his phone, he recorded himself humming the elusive tune so he wouldn't forget it. No one was nearby to hear him.

As he went to sing more of it, the inspiration ended, but he'd captured the core of it, before putting his phone back in the pocket of his jeans.

It was a solid start. The first in a while. Something he really liked rather than just a filler song to make up the twelve numbers on the album.

Walking back to the cabin, another part of the song drifted through his thoughts.

When he went inside, he sat down at his keyboard and began to play, recording as he went along. Again, the inspiration faded, but he had the bones of a song he could work on. This was often how his creative process worked. Nothing new in that. But the song's melody had more potential than anything he'd written for a long time.

He played around with the song, trying to figure out where the melody would lead him, and lost track of the time. It was only when he noticed the amber glow of the fading sun cast a warmth through the windows of the cabin that he realised he'd soon need to get kilted up for the ceilidh.

The crafting bee ladies had agreed to meet up slightly early at the castle so they could see the piano bar before heading through to the ceilidh night.

All of them were wearing dresses or a skirt and blouse ensemble suitable for the party. Many of them had dressmaking skills and had made their own outfits.

Sylvia wore a knee–length, tartan dress in a lightweight fabric, like a silk chiffon. It felt cool enough for the dancing, and had a full skirt. Her black ballet–style pumps were easy to dance in.

Aileen had sewn her own tartan wrap skirt and wore it with a short sleeve white blouse.

Others wore variations of dresses with a nod to tartan either by wearing a tartan sash with a plain dress, or a tartan pin on a blouse. Comfy shoes were essential, and as they attended the regular ceilidh dances at the castle, they all had dresses, skirts and tops to mix and match, and accessories suitable for the parties.

Jessy, although officially on duty that night, was there with them and switched on the chandeliers in the piano bar.

The ladies gathered together, admiring the baby grand.

'What a beautiful instrument,' Etta said, gazing at the piano.

'Play something so we can hear it,' Jessy encouraged Sylvia.

'I don't want to clash with the ceilidh music,' said Sylvia.

Jessy pulled the lounge doors shut. 'No one is there yet. Chef's just setting up the buffet. Most guests are in their rooms getting dressed.'

'Go on,' Muira encouraged Sylvia. 'Play a wee something for us before the ceilidh starts.'

Sylvia had brought some sheet music with her and selected a piece. She set it up on the piano and sat down to play. 'This is a classic rhapsody.'

As Sylvia began to play, filling the room with the romantic resonance, the ladies gathered round, enthralled.

Muira wiped away a tear as she listened to Sylvia playing, remembering the talent her niece had, and still retained. And seeing the looks on the faces of the ladies. Whatever they'd expected to hear, Sylvia had exceeded their expectations.

Apart from the music, there was a stunned silence as they listened to her play for them.

The last few notes hung in the air as Sylvia finished playing and lifted her hands gracefully off the keys.

A round of applause erupted in the room, along with compliments on her playing.

'I've never heard a grand piano played for real, up close,' said Etta. 'It sounded wonderful, Sylvia.'

The other ladies were equally complimentary.

Sylvia stood up. 'I think having this piano bar in the castle is a great idea. I'm really looking forward to the opening night.'

'Gaven's organising it as soon as he can,' said Jessy. 'The new paintings were hung up today, and as far as I know, that's the last piece of decor needed.'

'Oliver's art is lovely,' Sylvia remarked, admiring the paintings.

The others agreed and went over for a closer look at the artwork.

After chatting for a little while longer, the ladies headed through to the function room for the ceilidh party.

'With it being such a warm night, there are plenty of fruit sorbets and ice cream served up on the buffet,' Jessy told them. 'Chef let me try the raspberry and strawberry sorbets. I can recommend them. They're made with locally grown fruit.'

The buffet included a variety of summer dishes from Scottish salmon to salads and light pastries both savoury and sweet. A bar provided refreshments, and tea and coffee were available too.

The patio doors were open wide, leading outside into the garden where tables and chairs were arranged for guests to enjoy a breath of air during the evening. Lanterns lit up the patio area, along with twinkle lights.

Ceilidh music had started to play in the background, and guests were arriving to enjoy the dancing.

Gaven was busy in the reception, welcoming guests and playing host to the ceilidh. He wore his kilt, shirt and waistcoat, and smiled when he saw Laurie arriving.

'I'm glad you could make it,' Gaven said to him.

'Thanks for the invitation.'

Laurie wore a kilt in shades of deep blue tartan and a white Ghillie shirt that laced up the front.

'Oh, I have something for you,' Gaven suddenly remembered and stepped over behind the reception area. 'Sylvia gave me these for you.' He handed Laurie a paper bag from the sweet shop. 'Two chocolate robins.'

Laurie smiled as he accepted them.

'Tuck them in your sporran,' Gaven advised him. 'I've had half my sweeties munched by Walter and other staff,' he added, smiling. 'Though I've eaten plenty myself. But I do have a frying pan left.' He opened his sporran and showed Laurie a bag containing the last toffee lolly.

Laurie laughed. 'I haven't had one of those since I was a wee boy.'

'That's what I said when I saw them today in the sweet shop. I popped in to talk to Sylvia, and came out loaded with sweeties, including frying pans and your robins.'

'I'll pay for the robins,' Laurie offered.

'No, I bought my sweeties, but Sylvia gave me these for you as a gift.'

Laurie put them in his sporran. 'That was very thoughtful of her.'

Two women guests were excited to see the laird standing there in his kilt, and came over to him all smiles.

'We've never been to a ceilidh in a castle before,' one of the ladies said to Gaven. 'We're so excited.'

'I'm sure you'll enjoy yourselves,' said Gaven.

The other woman smiled at Gaven and Laurie. 'Tell me, what do you keep in your sporrans? I've always wanted to know.'

Gaven told her the truth. 'A frying pan.'

Laurie joined in the fun. 'My chocolate robins.'

'Oh! You're a pair of cheeky monkeys,' the woman said, laughing.

Giggling, the ladies walked away to join in the ceilidh.

Walter waved Gaven over. 'Are you ready to announce the opening reel?'

'I am,' said Gaven. 'Enjoy your night, Laurie.' And off he went, striding through to the function room to get the dancing started.

'Psst!' Walter hissed at Laurie. 'Can I have a wee word with you?'

Laurie frowned, thinking something was wrong. 'Yes, Walter.'

Out of earshot of everyone, Walter confided about Julia phoning the castle, and how the call had unfolded.

Laurie was concerned at first, thinking there was a chance she'd still arrive, but then he laughed when Walter told him about the sleeping bag.

They were still laughing when Sylvia walked out of the function room to the reception carrying the sheet music she'd brought with her.

Her heart jolted when she saw Laurie standing there looking like a tall, handsome kiltie. She hadn't expected to see him at the ceilidh, and not dressed to impress in a traditional kilt. The lace up ghillie shirt made him look like a sexy cover model, and she tried to hide the effect he had on her.

'Could you keep these safe for me behind the desk, please?' she said to Walter, handing him the music.

'Yes, I'll put them in the drawer for safe keeping.' Walter tucked them in the drawer. 'I thought I heard you playing in the piano bar.'

'I was just letting the bee members hear what the piano sounded like,' Sylvia explained.

And all the while Laurie stood there, lingering, eager to tell her how lovely she looked in her tartan dress, yet thinking he should keep such feelings to himself.

'I want to thank you for the chocolate robins,' he said instead. 'Gaven has just given them to me. He said they were a gift from you.'

'I promised I'd send them to the castle, so when Gaven was in the shop I gave them to him to bring up,' she explained.

Walter joined in the conversation. 'The laird shared his sweeties with me when we were hanging up Oliver's paintings in the piano bar. Other staff, including chef, snaffled them too.'

Sylvia laughed. 'Gaven came into the shop to chat to me, but as usual, he left with a load of sweeties he hadn't intended on buying. We tempt him every time he comes in.'

Sylvia tempted him every time he saw her, Laurie thought, wishing her every happiness with Gaven, while wishing too that she wasn't involved with the laird.

'I'd love to have a peek at the paintings,' said Laurie. 'And have another look at the piano bar. I never got a chance to see it properly.' Not when his attention was drawn to Sylvia laughing in the laird's arms.

Walter had to tend to a guest, leaving Sylvia standing with Laurie. 'I can show you,' she offered.

Laurie smiled. 'Thanks, and I'd love a look at the piano.'

Sylvia led the way, aware of how tall Laurie was. As tall as Gaven, and yet the effect was more potent from Laurie. She barely came up to his broad shoulders.

'I didn't expect to see you tonight,' she told him as they walked into the quiet piano bar that was still lit by the chandeliers. 'I wasn't sure if you liked ceilidh dancing, but obviously you're all kilted and keen.'

'I brought my kilt with me. I enjoy a ceilidh night, though I haven't been to one in a while.'

By now, they were walking over to the paintings.

'Gaven bought these from Oliver. He owns the art shop in the main street. He's a talented artist. I love these watercolours, especially the one of the piano. The dancing couple is gorgeous too.'

Laurie stood beside her admiring the artwork, admiring her too, though he kept telling himself that there was no reason for letting his feelings for her become any stronger. Her future was with the laird, not him.

CHAPTER SIX

Sylvia went over to the piano, still taken with the sheer class of it and the memories it invoked in her.

Laurie admired it. 'Do you still enjoy playing? I've never been away from playing keyboards and guitars for any length of time.'

'It all came back to me as if I'd never left it behind me,' she said wistfully, and sat down at the piano. Instinctively, she played a couple of chords, and then stopped.

'Don't stop,' Laurie urged her, and sat down beside her. The piano stool seated two, allowing for duets to be played.

'I don't want to play anything in case it disturbs the ceilidh. The walls of this lounge and the function room are probably so thick that the sounds won't transfer through, but until I know for sure from Gaven, I'd rather not risk it.'

'You're right, but play a couple of chords with me.' He placed his hands on the keys and played a few notes.

She felt his masculine strength close to her. It caused her heart to flutter. The ghillie shirt that laced up emphasised his strong, lean chest. His hands were elegant.

Sitting side by side with him, she touched the keys softly and played the chords at her part of the piano, while Laurie played his. To her surprise and delight they sounded in tune together.

'Perfect harmony,' he concluded, smiling at her.

She met his pale grey gaze up close for a moment and then concentrated on the keys. 'The tone of this baby grand is wonderful. It's rich and full, yet responds to a light touch.'

Laurie continued to play and glanced around him. 'The sound really resonates and fills the room.'

'I've always found it to be such an emotional sound. Some classical pieces sound so sad, and yet I don't feel melancholy, just swept up in the emotion of the feelings it evokes. When I'm playing entire songs on the piano, I become lost in the music and I don't think about anything else. It's relaxing yet uplifting.'

'I understand what you mean.'

'I do miss it,' she confessed, playing softly. 'I hadn't realised how much until I played again.'

'Would you consider performing again or anything like that?'

'No, I love the sweet shop and intend concentrating on that, and becoming a chocolatier. But I'll happily play the piano sometimes at the castle.'

'I suppose you don't have room for one where you stay.'

She shook her head. 'The accommodation is cosy, ideal for what I need, but a baby grand needs a room like this. Besides, a piano of this calibre is expensive. I'm not rich like Gaven...and you.'

He hit a wrong note.

'I didn't mean to sound envious of your wealth or success,' she was quick to add. 'I'm not. I don't think it equates to happiness. I do very well for myself, and I'm happy here.'

He believed her, but he chided himself for bringing up the topic. 'I'm sure you are. It was silly of me to suggest you'd have a piano like this at the cottage shop.'

'Maybe if I have a larger cottage one day, or a house, I'd consider having a piano. The renovated properties in this area are lovely. But I'm still fairly new to the village.'

They stopped playing, but continued to sit together and chat.

'Do you miss Edinburgh?' he said.

'No. I have plenty of fond memories of the city, but I'm glad I decided to move here. I'd split up with my boyfriend and the whole timing of making a fresh start was ideal.'

'Had you been dating long?'

'Two years. I'd been planning a future with him, while he'd been planning a future without me. It turned out that he was a slippery weasel, but I got over him easier knowing he wasn't the man for me after all.'

'You deserve better than a slippery weasel.'

'Thank you, Laurie.' She smiled at him, thinking perhaps she was revealing too much, and yet it felt easy to talk to him.

She played a few more notes as they continued to talk about their pasts and their presents.

'I thought I could trust him,' she said. 'Muira says my nature is too open and trusting.'

'You'll keep your guard up stronger now,' he remarked.

'No, I refuse to have the better parts of my nature tainted or diminished by someone with a rotten character.' She sounded adamant.

Laurie admired her attitude.

'But you'll need to be careful not to fall in love with the village,' she warned him lightly. 'A few guests who've come to stay at the castle have ended up moving here, like Neil the goldsmith. He makes exclusive jewellery. Some of his clients are top celebrities and Hollywood film stars like Bradley Goldsilver, Tiara Timberlane and Shaw Starlight. Neil is dating Penny now. Romance seems to be blossoming in the village lately. Etta says there are phases when love is in the air.'

Laurie knew he needed to be careful not to fall in love with Sylvia.

'I went exploring around the castle's estate today, and I loved all the nooks and crannies, like the natural pool. It made me want to go swimming.'

'I didn't know there was a pool. But I haven't seen half of the estate,' she said.

He sounded surprised. 'I thought Gaven would've given you the full tour.'

'No, he's a busy man. Often he's away in the city where he makes his business deals. Perhaps I'll have a wander around the estate while the weather is still warm and sunny and discover where this pool is hidden.'

'If you want, I'll show you. I intend enjoying the outdoor scenery while I'm here. I even came up with the beginnings of a new song this afternoon while I was out exploring.'

'Really? So you've ignited the fresh inspiration you need already. That's great.' She sounded happy for him.

His heart squeezed feeling her genuine warmth and friendliness. Then he played part of the new song on the piano.

She listened to the melody. 'That's lovely.'

'I played it on my keyboard and guitar when I got back to the cabin, but it sounds great on the piano.'

'The grandeur of the castle helps the acoustics. The sound reverberates so well in a room like this.'

'Would you feel at home living in the castle?' he dared to ask her.

Not knowing that he thought she was dating Gaven, she didn't pick up on this. 'No, I'd never want to actually live in a castle. It's nice to visit, but I'd feel like I was sharing my home with friendly strangers all the time, with the guests. Gaven was brought up here, so it's home to him, and he's upstairs in his turret with a romantic view of the loch.' She'd never been in the turret, but it was common knowledge that this was true.

'It sounds very romantic,' Laurie admitted, thinking she knew from personal experience.

'But I'd prefer a house.' She shrugged. 'And maybe I'd invest in a second–hand piano to play for the love of it.'

'Maybe you will,' he said.

'Play your new song again, Laurie, before we head through to the ceilidh.'

He played it again for her.

'I love that melody,' she said wistfully.

'Have you written any songs?'

'No, it's not in me to create music, just to play it. Thanks for letting me hear your new song. I suppose that makes me the first one to listen to it.' She sounded delighted.

'It does. I don't usually let anyone hear my songs when they're still so raw.'

'But I'm a bad influence on you, Laurie,' she joked.

They stood up and he smiled playfully at her.

'What?' she said, looking up at him with those green eyes so full of curiosity.

'I've got the chocolate robins in my sporran.'

She burst out laughing. 'Have you?'

He unbuckled his sporran and showed them to her.

She laughed again. 'This is definitely turning out to be a night to remember. Hearing your new song. And hiding chocolate robins in your sporran.'

'The night is young, Sylvia,' he said, leading her out of the piano bar towards the function room where the ceilidh music played loud and lively.

Several people noticed them walking in together.

Etta nudged Muira. 'Sylvia and Laurie look happy together.'

Muira agreed. 'They were probably playing the piano.'

'Yes, but I'm sensing a wee bit of romance in the air,' Etta added, smiling.

Muira did too. 'I know she thinks he's handsome, but she said she's not interested in a summer fling. And that's all it would be. She has no intention of leaving the village, and he has his successful life to go back to in Edinburgh.'

Etta nodded thoughtfully. 'But you never know...'

Aileen came over to Etta and Muira. 'I was wondering where Sylvia was, but I see she's been in Laurie's company. They make a fine couple. Not that I'm hinting that they are, or will be. I'm just saying.'

Gaven came over to them. 'Are you enjoying your evening, ladies?'

'We are,' said Etta. 'We've been jigging to all the dances and we were about to head over to the buffet.'

'There are plenty of refreshments and chef has laid on a tempting selection of dishes,' Gaven said, and then headed on to tend to other guests.

'Oh, look,' said Muira. 'Laurie is leading Sylvia on to the dance floor for the next reel.'

'He's a fine looking man in his kilt,' Etta commented. 'So is the laird, but they're two different types. Gaven looks like he belongs in a classic castle.'

'Wearing that ghillie shirt, Laurie looks like a cover model, one of those sexy, romantic hero sorts,' Aileen remarked.

They all agreed.

'I didn't expect Laurie to turn up wearing a kilt,' Muira confessed. 'Sylvia didn't even think he'd be at the ceilidh.'

'Laurie is just full of surprises,' said Etta.

'He's a good dancer,' Muira remarked. 'Clearly he's been to a few ceilidhs and knows the steps.'

The ladies then headed to the buffet, chatting about Sylvia and Laurie.

Gaven joined in the dancing, and as the reel came to a close, he ended up partnered with Sylvia for the next dance.

Laurie stepped aside to let Gaven dance with Sylvia. He didn't want to look like he was making a play for the laird's girl and went over to the buffet.

He ate a savoury pastry, unaware he was standing beside Etta and the other crafting bee ladies.

'Hello, Laurie, I'm Etta.' She introduced herself and the others. 'This is Muira, Aileen, Penny and Jessy.'

'I'm supposed to be working,' Jessy told him. 'But I'm joining in with some of the dancing.'

'And I'm Sylvia's aunt,' said Muira.

Laurie smiled at them as he finished eating the pastry. 'It's great to meet you all. I feel I know you from the radio show.'

'Were you playing the piano with Sylvia?' Jessy said to him.

'A bit. We didn't want to disturb the ceilidh,' he explained. 'I was impressed with the piano, and I'd love to hear Sylvia play an entire song.'

'Gaven's asked her to play at the opening night of the piano bar,' Muira told him. 'You'll hear her then if you come along.'

'I wouldn't miss it,' Laurie assured Muira.

'How are you settling in at the cabin?' Jessy said to him.

'Great. It's a beautiful cabin and I had a walk around the estate today, enjoying the countryside. Now I'm at the ceilidh.' He smiled. 'And I thought I had a busy life in the city.'

84

The ladies laughed.

'People are always surprised to find that our wee village is a hive of activity,' said Jessy.

'We're all back here at the castle tomorrow night for our crafting bee,' Etta added.

'What crafts will you be up to?' he said. 'I know from the radio that you were holding a knitting bee in your cottage. Are most of you knitters?'

'We are,' said Etta. 'Plus we're into quilting, embroidery, dressmaking, sewing and mending, all sorts of crafts.'

'My grandmother was a keen knitter,' Laurie revealed. 'She always knitted me great jumpers for the winter.'

'Etta's knitting a Fair Isle jumper for Mullcairn,' Jessy told him.

'I'll be working on finishing that at the bee night.' Etta explained about Mullcairn wanting the jumper. 'I'm adding wee extras like a scarf and woolly hat for him.'

'Lucky man,' said Laurie.

'I'd be happy to knit something for you,' Etta offered.

'A Fair Isle jumper would be nice,' he said. 'Do you sell your knitting online?'

'Yes.' Etta told him the name of her website.

Laurie pulled out his phone, and to their surprise and delight checked out Etta's jumpers and other knitted items.

'I like that jumper there. The Fair Isle in shades of grey. Is it for sale?'

Etta blinked. 'Eh, yes. It's a man's large size.'

'Sold.' Laurie smiled at Etta as he bought it there and then.

He continued to view the website. 'Is that a man's Aran jumper?'

'Yes,' Etta confirmed. 'A traditional cream Aran knit cable pattern.'

'I'd like that too.' He made the transaction on his phone.

'I'll bring the jumpers with me tomorrow night,' said Etta, taken aback by the sales.

'Perfect.' He smiled, pleased.

'Right, what's going on here?' Walter said jokingly as he approached them. 'Are you lot ganging up on poor Laurie?'

Laurie played along. 'They're forcing me to buy new jumpers.'

'Oh, they're wicked,' said Walter.

The ladies laughed.

'Next, they'll be forcing me to have some of that delicious looking ice cream,' Laurie added.

'You'll have to try chef's special Scottish raspberry ice cream,' Jessy insisted, joining in the fun.

'If I must.' Laurie laughed and helped himself.

They were all laughing and enjoying the buffet when Gaven came over to them.

'You lot seem to be enjoying yourselves,' Gaven commented.

'The buffet is tasty,' Laurie said to him.

'It'll give you energy to join in the dancing,' said Gaven.

Laurie laughed. 'Was that a subtle hint?'

'Nothing subtle about it. Come on,' Gaven gestured to him. 'I'm rounding up the lads for a fast–moving reel. If you're up for it.'

Laurie spooned up the last of the ice cream and put the empty dish down. 'I am.'

'Come on, you too Walter,' said Gaven.

The men gathered in a strong circle, and a rousing song began. And they were off, whirling around the floor, kilts swinging wildly, cheering as they danced. The ladies stood at the edges, clapping in time to the music, and then after a few minutes they joined in too.

Somewhere in the dance, Laurie saw Sylvia, and managed to wangle his way through the whirlwind until he was near her.

'It's a wild night,' Laurie called to her.

Sylvia smiled and nodded. 'Are you having fun?'

'Tons of fun.' His face showed that he was. In the company of new friends, he felt more at ease than he had in a long time. He remembered Sylvia's warning. He'd certainly need to be careful not to fall in love with the village. In barely a day, he felt his world had opened up in the small community. Something he hadn't anticipated.

Clasping hands with Sylvia, she felt his strength almost sweep her off her feet as they danced. She giggled at him.

'Sorry, Sylvia,' Laurie shouted over the loud, lively music.

She giggled again, and then she was gone, pulled into the next part of the dance by Gaven.

Laurie danced with Etta, then Aileen, Muira, all the ladies in turn, until the music finally stopped and everyone stood and applauded.

A slower dance followed, and Laurie frowned as he watched Gaven walk past Sylvia and dance with another lady. Seeing Sylvia about to leave the dance floor, Laurie clasped her hand.

'Do you want to dance with me?' he said.

She kept her hand in his as she replied. 'Yes. This one is a lot slower, so you won't risk sweeping me off my feet.'

He wished he could, in more ways than one. She looked lovely, and every time she smiled at him, he felt his heart was in jeopardy.

They danced around the floor to the country–style waltz. The lighting was dimmed to create a romantic atmosphere, allowing couples a few minutes to catch their breath before the ceilidh kicked into high gear again.

Wearing her ballet pumps, Sylvia was aware of how tall Laurie was as he held her in his arms.

'Etta and the ladies were saying they're attending their crafting bee at the castle tomorrow night,' he said. 'Will you be coming along?'

'I'll be there. I'm attempting to learn needle felting. My aunt is teaching me. I'm making a robin. At the moment, his beak is wonky, but I'm hoping to work on him at the crafting night.'

'I'm sure you'll make a great job of him.'

'Gaven says he wants to have the opening of the piano bar the night after the crafting bee. Apparently, guests are eager to see the piano and use the new bar.'

'You'll be playing at the opening,' he said hopefully.

'I will. I've told Gaven I'll play a sonata, a rhapsody and a concerto.'

'Impressive line up. I'm looking forward to hearing you play.'

'I'll add a couple of popular songs, contemporary numbers as well,' she said. 'And there will be a special cocktail menu.'

'Cocktails and classical music at the castle.' He nodded as he said this. 'It sounds as if we're in for a really special evening.'

'Have you tried the buffet tonight?'

'Yes, but I did more talking than eating. What about you?'

'I haven't had a chance since I arrived.'

'Would you like to go over and get something to eat now?' he offered.

Sylvia nodded. 'I skipped dinner because I knew I'd be coming to the ceilidh.'

Laurie escorted her over to the buffet where they selected savoury and sweet items and cold, refreshing drinks.

'Can we sit outside on the patio?' she said. 'It looks magical all done up with lanterns and fairy lights.'

'Yes, it's a lovely evening.' He led the way and they sat down at a table under the glow of the lights with the clear, star–sprinkled sky arching above them.

'I trust that Gaven won't mind that we're sitting out here together,' he said.

Sylvia frowned. 'Why would Gaven mind? The patio is set up for guests to enjoy the fresh night air.'

'I just meant that I'm out here with you.'

She still didn't get it. 'Why shouldn't you be? You're a guest at the castle.'

'But you're the laird's girlfriend.'

CHAPTER SEVEN

'I'm not the laird's girlfriend!' Sylvia told Laurie.

The news hit Laurie in two waves in quick succession. The first — she's not dating Gaven! The second — was she dating someone else?

'I'm not dating anyone,' Sylvia clarified, taking care of his second thought.

'When Gaven was holding you in his arms in the piano bar, I assumed...' His words trailed off.

'No, we were only carrying on. I'd gone up the ladder to adjust the lighting, my shoe came off and Gaven lifted me down,' she explained.

'Oh,' he said, the realisation kicking in.

'We're just friends. There's no romance between us. He's got a sweet tooth and loves my sweets from the shop, but the laird doesn't love me. I don't think he's in love with any of the local ladies. He seems to be all about business, running the castle, adding the cabins to the estate. The creative breaks are a new addition to the castle, and he's busy with that.'

The dots that he'd joined in his mind started to scatter like marbles. 'So you're really just playing the piano at the opening night because...'

'Because I can play the piano.'

Laurie felt a surge of excitement. 'That's wonderful. I mean, I understand now,' he corrected himself quickly, not wanting to let her know how much he liked her.

'Will we eat our food and then join in the dancing again?'

His appetite ignited. 'Yes, this looks delicious, and I didn't have lunch or dinner.' He couldn't hide the delight in his voice, thinking that maybe...maybe there was a chance for him to get involved with Sylvia.

She smiled over at him. 'You seem as if there something you're not telling me?'

'No,' he lied, and tucked into his food, avoiding her gaze.

'I think you're telling fibs.'

He shrugged his shoulders and continued to focus on his food.

She let it go. Whatever was on his mind she was sure she'd find out soon. It was difficult to keep secrets in the close knit community of the village.

'I'm eager to try one of the chocolate robins,' he said, changing the conversation.

'Go ahead.'

He dug one out of his sporran, trying not to laugh. 'Are they a special recipe? I noticed you have a few specialities on your shop's website.'

Sylvia smiled knowingly. 'Is that how you knew it was me when you first saw me with the laird?'

'Guilty as charged,' he admitted. 'I saw your picture on the shop's profile.'

'I had a nosey at your website during the radio show,' she confessed. 'I do know some of your songs. I've heard them played, but I wasn't familiar with you. I hope you're not offended that I didn't really know you.'

'Not at all. I'm not infamous, thankfully,' he joked with her.

She smiled at him. 'I imagine you're used to being feted by fans.'

'Fans of my music, those that turn up to my concerts, recognise me, but a lot of the time I fly below the radar depending on the company I keep.'

'Do you enjoy performing live in front of such large audiences?'

'Yes and no. I like the instant reaction from the audience, feeling the connection with them, but despite what I appear to be, I'm actually quite a private person.'

'I get that.'

He believed she did.

'Did you play to audiences often?' he said.

'I had three different music teachers over the years to expand my skill range,' she explained. 'They all encouraged me to take part in any competitions or performances available. I was very young when I first played the piano at a Christmas event in the city. It was an amateur festive event, but as I was just a wee girl, I thought it was great fun and wasn't nervous. So as I grew up I never really felt nervous when playing to an audience.'

'When did you stop playing?'

'In my teens. I played with an orchestra at a theatre, then I let the music go and concentrated on training in baking and making sweets. I'd loved baking since I was a wee girl, so it wasn't such a wild swing in my career choice.'

Laurie bit into the chocolate robin. 'Mmmm, lovely rich chocolate. I can understand why these are popular.'

'The chocolate has a mix of three flavours. I enjoy creating new blends.'

'It tastes like toffee liqueur and there's a hint of extra sweetness.' He continued to eat the robin.

'Honey, straight from the local beekeeper. The other ingredients are a guarded secret.'

'I won't ask, I'll just enjoy the chocolate.'

'Are you two dancing or sitting chomping chocolate all night?' Walter called out to them from the function room.

They smiled and stood up.

'Blame Sylvia,' said Laurie. 'She's been forcing me to eat chocolate.'

'She's a wee rascal. I had to help Gaven finish off the last bag of his sweeties. I assume he wanted me to do that because he'd left them behind reception.'

'Fair dibs,' Laurie told him.

Sylvia laughed. 'Gaven can always rely on you to help him out when it comes to eating sweeties.'

'Oh, yes,' Walter agreed.

Sylvia and Laurie followed Walter back into the hub of the ceilidh.

'Are you up for dancing some more with me?' Laurie said to her.

'Now that I'm not dating the laird you mean?'

Pulling her into hold, Laurie danced her into the lively jig, and for the rest of the evening they danced with each other more than with anyone else.

As the evening wore on, Sylvia chatted to Muira, Etta and Aileen as they sat outside on the patio while Laurie spoke to some of the other guests.

Sylvia sipped an iced lemonade and confided to them about Laurie's misunderstanding.

Muira looked surprised. 'Laurie thought you were dating the laird?'

'He did, but I've told him I'm not.'

Etta smirked. 'Is that why Laurie's got a spring in his sporran now?'

The ladies giggled.

'Etta!' Sylvia scolded her jokingly.

Etta shrugged. 'Well, he seems a wee bit happier now than he was earlier.'

'You've danced with Laurie a fair few times tonight,' Aileen commented to Sylvia.

Jessy had joined them for a breath of air. 'I wasn't going to say, but...Laurie's ex–girlfriend, Julia, is planning on making a comeback in his life now that she's split up with her latest squeeze.'

Sylvia didn't like the feeling that shot through her. She wasn't the jealous type, and she certainly didn't envisage getting seriously involved with Laurie. The reaction to the mention of his former girlfriend caught her off–guard.

'She'd sent Laurie a message saying she wanted to see him and was planning to come to the castle this evening,' Jessy elaborated.

'Is she here?' said Sylvia.

'No, she phoned up to book a room, but Walter knew the score and had promised Laurie he'd deal with the matter.' Jessy told them the details. 'But please don't say anything.'

The ladies nodded, assuring her they wouldn't.

'So what happened?' Etta wanted to know.

'She got a dose of Walter on the phone,' said Jessy.

'I suppose she's not coming to the castle then,' Etta surmised.

'Eh, no, she's not,' Jessy confirmed, trying to stifle a giggle.

'But she's obviously interested in getting back together with Laurie,' said Sylvia.

'She was well miffed,' Jessy revealed. 'She'd heard Laurie on the radio and knew he was working on a new album.'

Aileen had looked up pictures of Laurie and Julia on her phone. She held it up for them to read the gossip. 'They split up during his last tour. She'd ditched him for another celebrity. It was splashed across the gossip columns.'

'She's beautiful,' Sylvia remarked.

'A cold beauty,' Etta assessed. 'But a man like Laurie is bound to have a public past. Don't let it stop you getting to know him better, Sylvia.'

'As I've said before, I'm not looking for romance at the moment,' Sylvia reminded them. 'I'm happy as I am.'

'I know, but you should keep your options open,' said Jessy.

Muira nodded. 'You should, Sylvia. Laurie seems very nice. Just because you've been dancing with him, it doesn't mean that you need to get completely involved. Keep things light and friendly and see how it goes.'

'I'll think about it,' Sylvia said, wishing that things weren't complicated from the start. First, he'd thought she was dating Gaven. Now his ex–girlfriend was perhaps still on the scene.

'Join in everyone for the final dance of the evening!' Gaven announced from inside.

'Come on,' Jessy urged them. 'Let's kick up our heels.'

The ladies hurried inside as the music began, joining hands in a fast–moving circle reel.

Dancing between Muira and Aileen, Sylvia smiled over at Laurie as everyone whirled around the dance floor.

As the music finally stopped, guests clapped and cheered. Then everyone started to file out of the function room to their guest accommodation, or to their homes in the village.

Laurie waylaid Sylvia at the entrance to the castle as she was leaving.

'Are you free to join me tomorrow to take a walk to the outdoor pool?' he said.

Sylvia hesitated. 'I'm busy at the sweet shop. I don't want to leave Muira to do all the work.' Part truth, part excuse.

Laurie nodded that he understood and didn't pressure her. 'Thanks for dancing with me. I had a great time.' He waved and then walked away, heading to his cabin.

Muira and the other ladies overheard them.

'Don't miss out on having a nice day with Laurie,' Muira said to Sylvia. 'You're always working hard. I can manage the shop tomorrow.'

'Are you sure?' Sylvia said to her aunt, then glanced at Laurie walking away from the castle.

Muira nudged her encouragingly. 'Yes.'

Taking a deep breath, Sylvia called after him. 'Laurie!'

He stopped and glanced back at her lit up in the entrance.

'Can I change my mind?'

'Yes,' he said.

She smiled at him. 'I'll see you in the morning around ten.'

He smiled back, waved and then walked on into the night.

'Oooh! A date with Laurie,' Aileen said to Sylvia.

Sylvia blushed. 'It's not a date. He's just showing me a part of the estate.'

The ladies giggled, causing Sylvia to blush even more.

They piled into two cars and were each dropped off home.

Sylvia wandered through the sweet shop by the glow of the display lights, and got ready for bed.

Lying there looking out the window at the night sky, she rewound the events of the ceilidh. What an evening. And what a morning she'd inveigled herself into. But it wasn't a date, she told herself firmly. Definitely not a date. She was still trying to convince herself of this as she fell sound asleep.

The morning dawned bright and sunny. Sylvia drove up to the castle, planning to pop in and tell Gaven to expect a parcel. In all the excitement of the ceilidh, she'd forgotten to tell him that she'd ordered the sheet music. She parked her car outside the castle and headed towards the entrance.

She wore a ditsy print floral skirt and a white, short–sleeve blouse. A pretty but cool outfit and comfy shoes suitable for walking through the estate. She'd washed and dried her hair and it hung in silky waves around her shoulders.

The aroma of breakfasts being served to guests made her wish she'd had more than a cup of tea. But her stomach had been filled with butterflies of excitement as she got ready early in the morning.

She'd been up extra early to make nougat, fudge and tablet, and pack the online sweet orders that had come in overnight. Although her aunt was quite capable of handling this, she wanted to help with the work before skiving off to meet up with Laurie.

Walter and Gaven were chatting in reception and smiled when they saw her walk in.

'Morning, Sylvia,' said Gaven. 'I hear you're going exploring with Laurie.'

'Yes, I am.' She wondered how he knew.

'Laurie asked for an early morning wake–up call to his cabin,' Walter explained. 'He didn't want to sleep in as he was taking you on a tour to the estate's wee pool.'

Sylvia smiled and tried not to blush. 'Before I forget, keep a lookout for a parcel arriving today.'

Gaven frowned. 'A parcel?'

'It's a bargain bundle of sheet music,' she said. 'A selection of classical pieces and contemporary songs. I saw it for sale online and bought it. I gave the castle's address for the delivery.'

Gaven looked thrilled. 'Thank you. Let me know how much and I'll settle up with you.'

'No, it was a real bargain. I bought it for you, for the piano bar.'

Gaven went to insist on paying her, but Sylvia refused.

'That's very kind of you,' Gaven told her, taken aback.

'Okay, I'm heading off into the wild,' she said chirpily. 'Where exactly is Laurie's cabin?'

Walter handed her a leaflet from the reception desk. A map of the cabins was printed on the back of it. 'He's staying in that one there.'

'Would you like me to walk over with you?' Gaven offered.

'No, I'll follow the map.' Taking it with her, she waved and headed outside into the warm morning sunlight.

Laurie checked the time. He'd been up extra early, showered, tidied the already tidy cabin for Sylvia arriving, and packed away the groceries that Walter had delivered. Everything was set. He told himself to calm down. He didn't usually react like this. It was probably the overspill from the excitement of the ceilidh night.

He wore a white shirt, jeans and sturdy walking boots.

Peering out the window, he kept a lookout for Sylvia.

He checked the time again. Almost ten. No sign of her. Maybe in the light of day she'd changed her mind.

He checked his phone too in case she'd messaged him. They'd exchanged numbers at some point during the ceilidh. No message. No sign of—

There she was! Walking towards the cabin looking lovely in her pretty summery outfit, her hair shining like barley sugar again in the sunlight.

He was excited. But he was in trouble. He liked Sylvia. Really liked her. Though she'd made it clear she wasn't interested in romance at the moment. She'd mentioned it when they'd been chatting the night before.

Sylvia waved, seeing him peering out the window.

He stepped back, feeling caught, and went over and opened the cabin door to welcome her in.

'I hoped you hadn't changed your mind or become too busy at the sweet shop.'

'No, I'd popped into the castle to tell Gaven and Walter to expect a parcel of sheet music.'

'Come in.' He stepped aside so she could enter.

'Wow! This is gorgeous. No wonder it's called a luxury cabin.'

'My thoughts exactly when I arrived.'

She noticed the keyboard and guitars. 'You're all set up for playing your music I see.' She studied the keyboard.

'Have you ever played keyboards?'

'No, only piano.'

'Sit down and have a go,' he encouraged her.

Sylvia needed no encouragement. 'I've always wanted to try playing on a keyboard.' Placing her hands on the keys, she began to play.

'You're a natural,' he said.

'It sounds so different from the piano, and yet, it feels familiar.' She continued playing and looked around. 'Where's you sheet music?'

'I've been working on the new song, so I'd just been recording that on the playback.'

'Oh, right.'

He scrabbled to find some of his sheet music in his case. 'Here's a couple of pieces you can try. They're not classical though.'

She took them and set them up in front of her, and then reading the notes, she started to play the songs.

'What song is this? I've never played anything like this before, but it sounds great,' she said.

'It's one of mine, from my last album.'

'I love it.' She then played the other song. 'I suppose this is another one of your songs.'

'It is, though it sounds like a masterpiece when you play it.'

She smiled up at him. 'You're flattering me.'

'I'm telling you the truth. You play so differently from me. I'd never have thought that, but hearing your take on the song makes me want to up my game.'

'Nonsense. You're already at the top of your game, Laurie.'

He listened while she continued playing.

'Aren't you going to sing along?' she said. 'I can't sing for toffee.'

'I bet you have a sweet voice.'

'Nope. Singing and song writing aren't my forte. Just playing the piano.'

'And now a keyboard.'

She laughed. 'Don't let me get my hands on your guitars.'

'You play guitar?'

'No. I wouldn't know my frets from my strings,' she confessed.

Laurie lifted up his acoustic guitar. 'Try it.'

Taking up the offer, she stopped playing the keyboard and accepted the guitar.

He put the strap gently around her neck to support the weight of it.

His closeness made her heart flutter. His scent was clean, fresh, as if he'd just showered and shaved, and he had a hint of manly cologne.

'Do I strum it or pluck it?' she said.

Laurie's touch ignited her senses as he guided her hands, showing her how to hold the guitar, and then try a fretting technique and strumming.

'This feels so different than I'd imagined playing a guitar would be. I like the resonance, but it's quite hard for me to play.'

Laurie placed his hands on hers to stop her. 'It takes practise, but I don't want you straining your fingers. You've a sonata, rhapsody and concerto to play for the opening night.'

His calm strength stilled her hands, but stirred her heart. 'You remembered.'

He nodded, and took charge of the guitar, placing it back on the stand.

'Try the keyboard again,' he said.

'Only if you sing this time.'

'Okay.'

She sat back down and started to play while he sang.

Together their music filled the cabin.

The sun was shining bright outside, but as far as Laurie was concerned, the light inside the cabin was winning.

CHAPTER EIGHT

Sylvia finished playing the song in time with Laurie's singing, bringing the music to a cheerful conclusion.

She stood up. 'I get lost in the music when I'm playing, but I've never accompanied someone like you singing along.' She glanced out the window. 'We'd better get going to make the most of the morning.'

Laurie picked up a small rucksack he'd packed. 'I made a flask of tea and sandwiches. I thought we could have a makeshift picnic when we're out. Walter dropped off fresh groceries. I hope you like cheese, tomato and salad sandwiches. I saw that you enjoyed those type of things at the buffet.'

'Yes, that's ideal.' She dug into her bag and brought out a bag of sweets. 'My contribution to our outing.'

He peered in the bag and stole a chocolate toffee.

She picked a strawberry cream.

Eating their sweets, they headed outside into the warm sunshine.

Any hint of a breeze was shielded by the trees as they ventured off along a narrow path leading away from the cabin. The path soon disappeared under the lush grass, and she relied on Laurie to know what direction they were heading.

'Is Muira holding the fort at the sweet shop today?' he said as they walked side by side.

'Yes, I told her I'd be back in the afternoon to help pack the day's orders and take them to the post office. I got up early to pack the orders that had come in overnight. There were more than usual, so I'm glad I didn't leave my aunt to deal with them on her own. I'm guessing the extra customers are coming from people who tuned in to the radio show. They'll tail off once the buzz fades, but it was a handy increase in sales.'

'Does the sweet shop do quite well?'

'Yes, and I've tried to come up with new recipes. We sell a selection of favourite sweets, but customers like to try something new as well.'

'Even though Gaven warned me to steer clear of temptation, I must come down and have a browse in the sweet shop.'

'You'll be made welcome. As a first–time customer, you'll be given a taste tour of our top–selling sweeties.'

'Book me in for a taste tour.'

'Pop down anytime.'

'I'll do that.'

Sylvia gazed up at the cobalt blue sky. 'This area of the Highlands is so beautiful in the summer. We're lucky to be shielded by the hills.'

'According to the castle's information, the summers stretch well into the autumn.'

'This is my first summer here, but it certainly feels like those long summers when I was a wee girl. Muira says the autumn is glorious, and we're planning a new range of sweets including chocolate–dipped toffee apples, chocolate leaves and little marzipan pumpkins.'

'I'll have some of those, especially a toffee apple.'

'Remember to give me your home address in Edinburgh and I'll post them to you.'

His smile faded. 'Yes, I'll be back to my hectic life in the city by then.'

'I'd say your life has been pretty hectic since you arrived here. You might be glad to get home to rest and relax.'

He shook his head. 'No, I think I'll miss the village.' He glanced at Sylvia. And her.

'You'll have your new songs to keep you busy in Edinburgh,' she reminded him. 'Being here has sparked your creativity already. Imagine how many hit songs you'll have by the time you're back home.'

'I do feel inspired here, and I've enjoyed working on the new song.'

'Do you write one song at a time, or does the inspiration scatter wildly to various tunes?'

'Once I start to hear a new melody, other tunes begin to spark by the time I've got the first song down. One ignites the other, and so on.'

'Like a musical domino effect.'

He grinned at her. 'I like that idea.'

'What about the lyrics?'

'The words are not my forte. I have to really work at the lyrics.'

'The song you sang in the cabin sounded quite poetic as if you were speaking from experience of having had your heart broken and mended.'

'It sort of is,' he admitted, but didn't elaborate.

She decided to pry. 'Was it about you and Julia?'

'No, actually it wasn't about anyone I was involved with. It's hard to explain, but when I was writing it, I remembered all the times I'd put my heart on the line and had it broken.' He shrugged, as if trying to lift the burden of these from his shoulders. 'Not that I've been romantically involved a lot. Despite my reputation, I've made more time for my music and little time for love. Maybe that's what's been my problem in finding true love.' He put the focus back on her. 'What about you? Apart from Mr Slippery Weasel?'

'Nothing to write home about. Or write songs about for that matter.'

'But do you want to settle down one day?'

'I do, but I have a penchant for falling for the wrong men. A domino effect of rotten choices in romance.'

'The odds are bound to change in your favour sometime.'

'I wish I was as assured as you. You make it seem plausible.'

'It is.'

She looked doubtful. 'Just roll the romance dice and take a chance on love.'

He shrugged. 'Romance doesn't come with a happy ever after guarantee, not in my world.'

Not in hers either she secretly agreed.

'I prefer to use the tactic of narrowing the odds in my favour,' she said.

'Has that worked out for you so far?' He wasn't being intentionally sharp. 'It certainly hasn't played out well for me.'

She shook her head. The short line of fallen dominoes attested to that.

'Few trusting hearts are without their scars,' he concluded.

No more was said about both their rocky roads to romance.

They came to a fork in the greenery where the trodden pathway of thick grass divided into two different routes.

'I think I headed this way,' he said, sounding unsure.

'Did you bring any flares with you in the rucksack?' she toyed with him. 'Just in case we need someone to rescue us from the wild.'

'It is pretty wild in the depths of the estate, but I'm up for taking a chance on route A.' He sounded full of adventure.

Sylvia matched him. 'Let's go. The worst that can happen is that we become totally lost and have to spend the night in the depths of the creepy forest.'

'That doesn't instil the least bit of confidence in me,' he said with a wry smile. 'And how do you know that the forest is creepy at night? Is there some misadventure you've had that you're not telling me about?'

She played along with him. 'No, I'm not the type to go creeping about a dark forest. But look at those thick evergreens in broad daylight. It's really dark in there during the day.'

'Thankfully, route A circumvents the depths of the forest,' he said, leading them along a pathway edged with wildflowers.

'I love that the estate has cultivated gardens, with archways of roses and jasmine, along with patches of wildflowers. Look at those forget–me–nots, foxgloves and Scottish bluebells.'

'You sound like you know your flowers. Are you a keen gardener?' he said.

'I'd like to be. I have a garden at the back of the cottage. Seeing those lanterns and twinkle lights at the castle last night has put me in the mood to add lights to my garden.' She turned the question back to him. 'Do you have a garden at your house in Edinburgh?'

'I have a garden that surrounds the property, but I pay a gardener to keep it tidy. Though since I bought the house a few years ago, I've barely had time to enjoy it properly.'

'Something to rectify when you get home.'

Every time she mentioned about him going home, he felt a stab of doubt. 'Yes,' he said.

'You don't sound so sure,' she remarked.

He took a long breath. 'It's where I live, but it's never felt like home. When I go on tour, I don't miss it like I should.'

'It's probably that your whole lifestyle is unsettled,' she suggested.

'I think it's more like I'm living in the wrong location.' He looked around him, but didn't say anything.

They walked on, searching for the route to the natural pool.

Sylvia breathed in the fragrant air. 'The castle's estate is wonderful. We haven't seen anyone, though I'm sure there are other guests venturing around.'

Laurie suddenly pointed to a dip in the pathway. 'The pool is over there. Come on.'

Leading the way through an area lush with greenery and wildflowers, they arrived at the natural pool.

The air had changed to a lighter floral fragrance, as if the pool watered down the intensity, creating a bubble of cool calm.

Trees shaded part of the pool, but the other part where a small waterfall trickled down the polished stones, shimmered in the bright sunlight.

Sylvia gasped. 'It's beautiful.' Far lovelier than she'd imagined.

The water was clear, filtered by the natural stones. Flowers grew around the edges, and she walked over and sat down on the soft, springy greenery.

Laurie joined her.

She trailed her fingers through the cool water. 'It's not too deep, but it'll be ideal for us skinny dipping.'

Laurie jolted. 'Skinny dipping!'

'Unless you've got your trunks on under your jeans.'

'No, I...eh, I didn't think we'd be going swimming.'

She forced herself to keep a straight face while winding him up. 'I never thought we'd traipse all the way here just for a quick paddle.' She kicked off her shoes and swung herself around so that her feet were in the water. 'Oooh! It feels great.' She stood up in the knee–deep water that almost touched the hem of her skirt and started to wade across it.

Laurie was still pondering the skinny dipping surprise. Was he up for it? He wasn't sure that he was. He wasn't sure if he wasn't.

Sylvia couldn't contain her laughter any longer. 'You should see your face. You're sooo serious.' She giggled, and he realised she'd been fooling with him.

'Why you little minx!' He laughed, and standing at the edge of the pool, he reached over, grabbed hold of her and lifted her up.

She squealed with surprise and delight. 'No, Laurie! Don't throw me in! I was just kidding.'

'I'm not. You're going in for a dook young lady.' He pretended that he was going to throw her in fully clothed.

She wrapped her arms around his shoulders and buried her head into him. 'Nooo!'

Feeling her nuzzle into him, his heart melted a little, a lot. She felt feminine and fragile, yet feisty and fun–filled. The combination made him want to kiss the breath from her. But he wouldn't dare compromise her trust.

He put her down gently at the side of the pool.

She breathed a sigh of relief and then swiped at him. 'Rascal!'

'Me? I'm not the skinny dipping troublemaker.'

They laughed, and for a moment, she forgot that they were fairly new acquaintances, for she felt at ease and happy with Laurie, as if she'd known him for longer.

And in the next moment, she almost let herself kiss those firm lips of his. He looked so handsome, it almost took her breath away.

The attraction between them was evident. He stepped back and ran a hand through his hair as if to brush away the temptation to kiss her and tell her how much he liked her.

'Would you like to have our picnic here?' he said, lifting up the rucksack where he'd discarded it.

Sylvia sat down at the edge of the pool and let her feet and legs dry in the sunshine. 'Yes, please. I've worked up quite an appetite. It must be all the fresh air and shenanigans.'

He poured two cups of tea from the flask and handed one to her. 'And trouble–making.'

Her wide green eyes blinked in fake offence. 'Who me?'

'Yes, you, Sylvia.'

She laughed and stole a treacle toffee from the bag.

'Sweets are for dessert. Sandwiches first.' He gave her a sandwich and took one for himself.

The chewy toffee slowed down her response, causing him to stifle a laugh.

'You look like you've swallowed a bee,' he said.

'I'm trying to chew this at speed so I can have my sandwich,' she mumbled.

He shook his head. 'I can't take you anywhere.'

'No one has said that to me since I was seven,' she told him.

'I doubt that,' he argued lightly. 'You're a bundle of mischief. I knew that the first time I heard you speak on the radio.'

She leaned back and observed him. 'Really?'

He took a bite of his sandwich and nodded.

'I thought you were sort of reticent and quiet,' she said.

'I'm still cringing at how grumpy I must've sounded at the start of the radio interview.'

Sylvia shook her head. 'No, you were too quiet to register as grumpy.'

'Thanks for making me feel even worse,' he joked.

She laughed. 'But it all worked out fine. Now here you are having tea and sandwiches in the sunshine.'

'Give me a piece of that treacle toffee,' he said.

'I thought it was for dessert,' she reminded him.

'I'm learning all your bad habits, Sylvia.'

Sipping their tea, they ate their sandwiches and the sweets, and chatted about everything and nothing again.

They enjoyed each other's company and formed an easy rapport. Laurie wondered if it was their mutual love of music that made them so in sync. Or maybe the music had little to do with their blossoming friendship, and it was really just due to the potential for love.

'It must be hard to keep coming up with new songs for your albums,' she remarked. 'I can't imagine creating any songs.'

'I try to keep a high bar for what songs make the final cut.'

'Your new song has hit potential. I keep rewinding that lovely melody.'

'That's great to know.' He sounded pleased.

'Will you be playing at the opening of the piano bar?' she said. 'Not your new song, but performing your other hits.'

'No, that's not been mentioned to me. I'm not the classical pianist. You are.'

She let it go. He was probably invited to play at most events he attended and just wanted to relax and enjoy the evening.

'I'm planning to get in some practise tonight when I'm at the crafting bee,' she told him.

'What's the hardest piece you'll be playing at the opening?'

'The concerto. But I played it for years and love the challenge it presents. Besides, it's not a performance evening. I'm just there providing background and helping promote the piano's capability. Gaven's taking photos to put up on the website to advertise the piano bar. I've agreed to be included in the pictures, so I'll have to think what dress to wear.'

'Whatever you choose, you'll look beautiful.' The compliment was out before he could curtail it.

Sylvia blushed.

Laurie swallowed down the remainder of his tea and put the cup and flask back in the rucksack.

Sylvia finished her tea and added her empty cup.

He busied himself collecting their sandwich wrapping and sweetie papers, stuffed them in the rucksack and slung it over his shoulder.

'Feel like heading over there?' He pointed to another part of the estate. 'I never got that far the last time.'

'I've never been there either.'

Heading together towards a stretch of open grassland sprinkled with wildflowers, they chatted about music and their love of the scenery all around them.

They stopped at a little wrought iron bridge over a narrow stream that appeared from out of the forest on the outskirts of the area and that disappeared into the distance.

Sylvia leaned over and peered down at the water that sparkled in the sunlight.

She blinked. 'I'm dazzled!'

So was he, Laurie thought to himself. By Sylvia. The more time he spent with her, the more he realised how much he liked her company.

He glanced around. 'Where do you think the stream starts, and where does it end?'

'Never mind. Beginnings and ends of things aren't usually the fun parts. It's everything that happens in the long, meandering middle that's usually the most exciting.'

'Maybe that's where I am,' he said thoughtfully. 'My career is established and now I'm here, working on the near future.'

'Muira says I need to take more time off from the shop. Days like this. I can't remember the last time I skived off work. Though making sweeties never feels like work. It can be quite relaxing stirring liquid toffee and pouring it into moulds to set. Or dipping apples in it.'

'You're tempting me with the thought of a toffee apple. Here's my address in Edinburgh in case I have to run off without ever giving it to you.' He sent it to her from his phone.

Her phone pinged as the message was received.

'What would cause you to run off?'

'Nothing I can think of at the moment.' He just wanted to make sure she had his address.

'I'll need to be heading back fairly soon,' she said with a reluctant sigh.

'Will Muira be busy at the shop?'

'No, she's very efficient at handling everything smoothly. She'll be cutting the tablet into squares, chatting to customers while serving them, and putting the kettle on for an afternoon cuppa.'

'Sounds sweet and relaxing.'

Sylvia nodded and swept her blonde hair back from her face as she felt the warmth of the sunshine.

'Could I tempt you to have a cup of tea at my cabin before you head back to the sweet shop?'

'I could be tempted.' In more ways than one. But she wasn't telling him that. Not now. Perhaps not ever.

They crossed the bridge and then circled back towards the direction of Laurie's cabin for a relaxing cup of afternoon tea.

The cabin was in view as they walked along the pathway leading back to it.

Sylvia's phone rang. She checked the caller.

'It's Muira,' she said to Laurie. 'She's probably double–checking that I'll be back soon.'

Laurie nodded as she took the call.

'Sylvia!' Muira's voice sounded shrill.

'What's wrong?' Sylvia said immediately. 'Is everything okay?'

'No, yes, definitely not,' Muira spluttered.

Chaos sounded in the background. Chatter, rattling of sweets being measured at speed on the scales, paper bags rustling. And voices sounding panicky.

'What's happening at the shop?' Sylvia said, hearing herself start to panic.

'It's jumping like jelly beans with customers!' Muira shouted to make herself heard over the melee. 'The sweet shop was mentioned in the local newspaper. We're on the front page with Gaven's castle. The headline story this week is us being featured on the radio show!'

'The sweet shop is talked about in the local newspaper?' Sylvia sounded delighted and surprised. 'That's great publicity.' The newspaper was based in one of the towns. It covered the local area and was published weekly.

'Yes, but I had to phone Etta to come and help me deal with customers. We're up to our aprons in jelly crocodiles and butterscotch. And we've run out of frying pans and chocolate robins.'

'Calm down, Muira. I'm on my way.'

Laurie caught the gist of the dilemma. 'Can I help?'

'Are you able to bag sweeties? Do you know your soor plooms from your aniseed balls? Your fizzy flying saucers from you cinder toffee?'

He didn't think so. 'Yes, absolutely.'

'Okay, let's go. My car is parked at the castle.'

'Jump in my car. I'll drive us down. It'll be quicker,' he offered.

Without hesitation, Sylvia got in and Laurie drove them out of the castle's estate, along the edge of the forest, past the loch and parked outside the sweet shop in the main street.

They jumped out and ran in together.

CHAPTER NINE

Laurie barely had time to take in the pretty shop's jars of sweets lining the shelves and the delicious aroma of everything from vanilla and strawberry to treacle and chocolate, before he was cast into the melee of the mix.

A customer was leaving with bags of sweets, and another two customers were being served by Muira while Etta bagged the orders at speed.

'Laurie's here to help us,' Sylvia announced, leading him through to the kitchen and grabbing a copy of the newspaper that was behind the counter on the way.

'Wash your hands and put on an apron,' Sylvia instructed him while she skim–read the front page story.

Laurie rolled his shirt sleeves up and scrubbed his hands while trying to peer at the paper.

He caught a glimpse of himself in one of the pictures, along with a photo of Mullcairn. The village's main street showed several shops, but highlighted the sweet shop. Inset was a picture of Sylvia taken from the shop's website. The photo he'd seen and admired. Gaven was pictured standing outside his castle.

The entire front page featured the news story explaining that Laurie had been interviewed live on the popular radio show by Mullcairn, and that local villagers became part of the chat during a phone–in.

The headline grabbed Sylvia's attention. *Sweet Music for local village on radio show!*

She read aloud the relevant snippets...

'*Laurie was interviewed by Mullcairn about his forthcoming album and his new single was played for the first time on the radio...*'

'*Members of the village's crafting bee were having a knitting night at Etta's cottage beside the loch...*'

'*Expert Etta phoned the radio show and took part in the live chat with Mullcairn...*'

'*Mullcairn says Etta is now knitting him a Fair Isle jumper...*'

'*Jovial Jessy, a key worker at the castle, joined the cheery phone–in, telling Laurie he'd enjoy his stay in the luxury cabin at the magnificent castle...*'

'*Local heartthrob, Gaven, the castle's laird, has bought a baby grand piano for his new piano bar that's opening soon...*'

'*Muira, owner of the village sweet shop, revealed that her niece and sweet maker at the shop, Sylvia, is a classically trained pianist...*'

Under her photo was a caption: *Secret pianist, sweet shop Sylvia.*

The story continued...

'*Sylvia flirted with trouble and challenged Laurie...*'

She gasped. 'I didn't challenge you to play the piano,' she said to Laurie as he dried his hands.

Laurie shrugged and smiled. 'Where are the aprons?'

Sylvia put the paper down as it was distracting her. Before she could tell him, Muira overheard and called through.

'Aileen handed in two of the new sweetie fabric aprons. Etta's wearing the last white one. The others are in the wash. Wear the new ones.'

Laurie unhooked the two sweet pattern aprons and held them up. 'What one do you want?'

Sylvia chose the pink background apron, leaving Laurie with the white and sweetie print.

Game for helping, he put it on and tied it. 'What do you want me to do first?'

Sylvia threw her apron on and washed her hands. 'Help Etta bag the sweeties.'

Multi–tasking, Sylvia became a whirlwind of activity, serving customers, showing Laurie what sweets to bag, weighing the amounts, checking the online orders and trying to keep up with the fast–moving melee.

Laurie concentrated on not dropping any sweets, but some were like marbles, and he ended up chasing them around the jar with his scoop.

'Dig in and catch what you can,' Sylvia advised him.

Laurie gave it a go and within three small scoops, he had the measured amount he needed.

Etta wrapped boxes of chocolates.

Laurie moved on to bagging the nut brittle and nougat.

'We're getting there,' said Muira. 'Less folk are coming in as it's nearing closing time.'

Sylvia nodded. 'If we can get the online orders packed and taken to the post office in time we'll have caught up with the everything.'

'Luckily, we'd ordered in plenty of sweeties and ingredients, so we're well enough stocked, and we can reorder tomorrow.' Muira bagged a scoop of bonbons.

'I'll make more tablet and anything else we've run out of,' Sylvia assured her.

'Thanks for mucking in, Laurie,' Muira said, sounding grateful.

'I'm happy to help.' His height was an advantage when they needed jars lifted down from the top shelves without using the step ladder.

Etta grinned at him. 'Are you having a nice relaxing break at our quiet wee village?'

Laurie burst out laughing. 'Oh, yes.'

'We did have a nice time meandering around the estate,' said Sylvia while continuing to pack the orders. 'Apart from when Laurie threatened to throw me into the wee pool fully clothed.'

'She'd tricked me into thinking we were going skinny dipping.' He defended his actions with a wink. 'I was just joining in the joke.'

'It sounds like you both had a lovely time,' said Muira. 'I'm sorry it ended in a frenzy of fizzy sherbet and cola cubes.'

'No one is going to believe us that you were working in the sweet shop,' Sylvia told him.

Laurie took out his phone and stood beside her. 'Come on you two,' he said to Muira and Etta.

The four of them stood close together while Laurie held his phone up. 'Smile and say sweeties.'

They all laughed and said in unison, 'Sweeties!'

Laurie showed them the photo. 'Proof if you need it.' He sent a copy to Sylvia.

'Thanks, Laurie,' said Sylvia. 'You look like a sweetie chef with your apron on.'

'I love the new aprons Aileen made for you,' Etta remarked.

Laurie looked surprised. 'Aileen made these? They look lovely.'

'We wanted aprons that promoted the sweet shop,' Sylvia explained. 'Aileen had this great fabric with two different colours of background. We ordered them both.'

'Aileen says she'll bring the other two aprons to the crafting bee tonight,' Muira told Sylvia.

'I don't think I'll go to the bee this evening,' said Sylvia. 'I'll stay here and make the sweets we've run out of.'

'No, you're not missing out on the crafting bee,' Muira said firmly. 'You can make them in the morning.'

'You planned to practise playing the concerto,' Laurie reminded her.

Sylvia sighed. 'You're right. I'll go. And I wonder if the newspaper story has caused the castle and other local shops to be buzzing with extra customers.'

'I've sold all my Fair Isle jumpers and I have orders for more,' said Etta. 'Don't worry, Laurie, I didn't sell yours. I'll bring them to the castle tonight. I've pressed and packed them.'

'I'm looking forward to wearing them, Etta,' he said.

'Do you need to go home to pack your orders and take them to the post office?' Sylvia said to Etta.

'No, I posted them on my way here,' Etta explained. 'But I'm going to be busy knitting the orders for more.'

'I can imagine the sparks will be flying off your knitting needles,' Laurie joked.

'They will tonight at the bee.' Etta sounded adamant. 'I'm determined to finish Mullcairn's jumper.'

'Bradoch from the bakery was in for chocolate buttons to decorate his cakes,' Muira told Sylvia. 'He said a lot of the wee shops in the main street have enjoyed a boost in sales due to the newspaper feature.'

'The main street was busy, as if it was Christmas,' Etta remarked. 'The story has really caught people's attention. Folk from the surrounding towns headed here, and others are checking out the village shops online and placing orders.'

'I've nearly finished the orders on my list,' Laurie announced.

'Well done,' said Sylvia.

'And I didn't snaffle any of the sweets,' he added.

'Snaffle what you want,' Sylvia told him. 'Consider it your taste tour.'

He threw her a mischievous smile. 'Really?'

'Yes.' Sylvia gestured to the jars on the shelves. 'Try whatever takes your fancy.'

Muira and Etta exchanged a smirk and giggled as they continued working.

'What are you two giggling at?' Sylvia said to them, knowing that they were hinting that there was an attraction between her and Laurie.

Muira kept her head down. 'Nothing.' She then checked the time. 'Oh, the post office will be closing soon. Grab whatever you can and let's get the orders away in the post.'

Sylvia didn't hesitate. She grabbed a couple of large bags that they used for carrying the orders and loaded them to the brim.

'Let me take them to the post office so you can get on with your work,' Laurie offered.

'Thanks,' said Sylvia. 'We have an arrangement with the postmaster. All you have to do is drop the parcels off at the post office. I'll phonc ahead and let him know you're popping along with them.'

'Where's the post office?' he said, taking his apron off and lifting the bags.

'At the far end of the main street.' Sylvia pointed in the direction.

'I won't be long,' he promised and headed out to his car and drove off with the parcels.

'He's very willing to help us,' Muira said as they continued working.

'Did you go swimming with him?' Etta wanted to know.

'No, I had a paddle, then we sat there enjoying a picnic. He'd made a flask of tea and sandwiches for us.'

Etta and Muira looked impressed.

'He really seems to like you,' said Muira.

Etta agreed.

'We get on well. We talk a lot about music, and he let me try playing his keyboard and guitar in his cabin.' Sylvia told them the details. 'I played and he sang. He's a great singer.'

'A romance is definitely brewing,' Muira commented.

Sylvia disagreed. 'I've made it clear to him that I'm not interested in romance at the moment, especially as he's only here for a wee while. So we're just keeping things on a friendly basis.'

'That's sensible,' Muira agreed. 'But you never know where things could lead.'

'He's heading home to Edinburgh after his break here,' said Sylvia. 'He's got a house there, and he needs to record his new songs at the recording studio in the city.'

They knew Sylvia didn't want to leave the village and live in Edinburgh, so they let it go and changed the conversation around to the crafting bee.

'I'm still knitting my lilac cardigan, so I'll be bringing that with me tonight,' said Muira. 'But I'll bring my needle felting too.'

'I'll be working on Mullcairn's Fair Isle jumper.' Etta looked pleased. 'I've nearly finished it.'

'I'm bringing my needle felting,' said Sylvia. 'I want to work on the robin.' She checked the time. 'If you two want to head home to get ready for this evening, I can tidy things up here in the shop.'

Refusing to leave Sylvia to do this on her own, Muira and Etta hurried up to clear away the jars that needed put back on the shelves and tidy up the bags and remnants of sugar crystals and stray chocolate buttons.

Between the three of them, they made short work of the task.

Muira and Etta had just left by the time Laurie arrived back from the post office.

'The parcels are all posted away on time,' he announced. 'Where's Muira and Etta?'

'They've gone home to get ready for the crafting bee,' Sylvia explained. 'They helped me clear up, so there's little to do except make myself an easy dinner and get ready too.'

He lingered, wondering if he should go, yet wanting to stay.

'You're welcome to stay if you want,' she offered. 'Dinner won't be anything fancy.'

'If you're okay with me hanging around...' He shrugged and smiled at her.

She locked the shop's front door and turned the sign to closed, then she led him through to her private kitchen.

'This is nice,' he said, looking around the quaint little cottage accommodation tucked at the back of the shop. He peered out the kitchen window at the garden.

Sylvia opened the door to let the air in. A mellow sun was fading in the blue sky that refused to surrender easily to the early evening glow.

Laurie stepped outside. 'Lanterns and twinkle lights would look great in your garden.'

'I think I'll buy a few strings of outdoor lights and drape them up. Sitting out here in the summer

127

evenings is very relaxing after a busy day, and I've always liked fairy lights and sparkle.'

He wandered further into the garden for a look around.

She watched him from the window as she planned what to make for dinner.

'Do you like pasta?' she called out to him.

'Yes, whatever you're having is fine by me. I'm not a picky eater.'

'Except when it comes to sweeties,' she said, putting a pan of water on the stove to cook the pasta. 'I saw you picking your favourite flavours from the mixed assortments.'

He spread his arms wide and laughed. 'I'm in a sweet shop, given carte blanche to try my favourites.'

'Did you enjoy your taste tour?' She opened a jar of pasta sauce and put the rich tomato, peppers and spicy sauce on to heat.'

He frowned. 'I think I need the full tour.'

Sylvia guffawed. 'Trust me, you tasted everything I'd have offered you, and a few extras.'

He shook his head. 'No, I'm sure I must've missed something.' Then he remembered. 'The frying pans. They were sold out. I've yet to try one of those.'

'Okay,' Sylvia conceded with a smile. 'I'll make sure you get one when I make more of them.'

He nodded and then wandered back in from the garden. 'Anything I can do to help?'

'Stir the sauce, while I set the table.'

Laurie stirred the savoury sauce, tempted to taste it, but then thought better of it and put the spoon away from his lips.

'Don't even think about it,' she warned him.

'I didn't.'

She shook her head at him and put two dinner plates on the table along with cutlery and napkins. The accessories in her kitchen were an eclectic mix of pretty prints and vintage style florals, from the patterns on the plates to the ditsy strawberry print curtains on the window.

He admired the decor. 'This is really nice.'

'The benefit of being a member of the crafting bee is that there's no shortage of items like these. We all make things for each other as gifts, and buy them too. Muira made the strawberry print curtains with fabric from Aileen's quilt shop. The oven gloves and tea towels have strawberries in the prints too. I bought them from one of the members.'

'I like the style of your kitchen. It feels cheery, bright and homely.'

'Etta knitted the pink tea cosy and a set of egg cosies for me as a welcoming present when I first moved in.'

'It was kind of her to come and help Muira today, especially when she could've got on with her knitting,' he remarked.

'It's the way of things around here, especially with the ladies of the crafting bee. We all look out for each other and rally round when needed. People have time for each other here even though we're often busy.'

'I have to say that I thought the pace of life here would be slow,' he admitted. 'But it's been an enjoyable and fascinating whirlwind since I arrived. To be fair, I thought I'd be holed up in my cabin most of the time, and going out for a walk in the estate for fresh air.'

'And here you are, inveigled in our mayhem.'

The look he gave her set her heart aflame. 'I can't remember a day recently when I've had so much fun. It's the most I've felt like myself from the past in a long time, before the fame and notoriety.' A smile formed on his oh so kissable lips. 'Working at the sweet shop is a memory I'll treasure for ever. Here, I'm just Laurie, not the well–known musician.'

He looked away and concentrated on stirring the sauce while she drained the pasta. 'The sauce is bubbling.'

Sylvia peered over. 'It's nice and hot. I'll serve up the pasta, you pour the sauce on, or I'll do it.'

'No, I'll do my bit. We'll work together. We make a great team.'

They did, she thought, feeling at home with Laurie, and yet reacting to having this tall, handsome man in her kitchen.

He set up the mugs while she made a pot of tea.

Sitting down at the kitchen table, they started to eat their dinner, enjoying the warm breeze blowing in from the garden and each other's company.

'When does your crafting bee night start?' he said.

'Seven, but we usually go along a bit early to set things up. Depending on how the evening goes, I'll head through to the piano bar to practise playing. Or I'll stay late after the bee night is finished.'

'When I finish dinner I'll head up to the cabin and let you get ready...but I'd be happy to drive you back up.'

'A lift would be handy as I've left my car at the castle.'

'That's settled then.' He tucked into his pasta.

'What are you up to this evening? I've taken up all of your day. Will you work on your new song?'

'Probably, but I wondered if I could hear you play tonight?'

'An audience of one?'

'An intrigued one.'

'Drop by if you want.'

'I won't put you off your practise?' he said.

'No, if you're okay listening to me.'

He looked pleased. 'It's a date.' Then he corrected himself. 'Not a date.'

Sylvia laughed.

'Phone me at the cabin when you're heading through to the piano bar and I'll come over,' he said.

'I will,' she assured him. 'Wish me luck on getting the concerto right.'

'You don't need luck, Sylvia. You're a talented pianist.'

'I enjoyed playing the keyboard.'

'You're welcome to play it again anytime.'

'I might take you up on that while you're here.'

And there it was again, that dagger of doubt, or disappointment, knowing that whatever friendship there was between them, he wasn't a permanent fixture in her world. Edinburgh loomed on the distant horizon. But it was there nonetheless.

'I haven't heard from Gaven,' she said. 'I hope the delivery of the sheet music arrived. He's probably been busy with people contacting the castle because of the story in the newspaper.'

'I feel I've caused ructions in the village by being interviewed on the radio.'

'As I've told you, people think the village is quaint and quiet, but there's always something going on.'

'The opening of the new piano bar is bound to attract even more attention,' said Laurie.

Sylvia nodded and took a sip of her tea, feeling the excitement building.

CHAPTER TEN

After Sylvia and Laurie finished dinner, she showed him through to the living room while she got ready for the crafting bee.

'Make yourself at home.' She gestured around the cosy living room, and then left him while she went into her bedroom to freshen up and change into a light blue chambray dress.

Laurie wandered around, taking everything in. The decor matched the kitchen's pretty vintage style with light beige walls, floral print sofa and chairs, quilted cushions and a dresser painted pastel pink where she kept her fabric and yarn stash and crafting items tucked tidily away.

Her craft bag was packed ready with the needle felting and the pink yarn for the socks she never got around to starting at the knitting night. The bag itself was a voluminous quilted design.

On the table near the window where she had her sewing machine, was the small, red, vintage suitcase where she kept her sheet music. The case was open and Laurie noticed the classical selection of songs.

He tilted his head to the side to read the top sheet, trying to hear the music in his head as he deciphered the notes.

'I see you have an impressive collection of sheet music,' he called through to her.

'I kept all my music. I was looking through them to find suitable pieces for the opening night,' she called back to him while she brushed her hair and touched up her makeup. 'Take a look if you want.'

He did, carefully peering at them so as not to disturb the order they were in. Sylvia had packed them neatly.

'I narrowed it down to a small selection. The ones on the top of the pile.' She walked through as she continued to explain. 'There are a couple of concerto pieces, three sonatas and two rhapsody choices.'

He admired her as she stood next to him. 'Will you play these tonight?'

'Yes, I thought I'd practise pieces of them, see how each one feels when played on the baby grand.'

'I notice you give priority to how the music feels rather than how it sounds.'

'I do. The acoustics of the room will obviously affect the sound, but at the heart of the music is how it feels.'

She lifted the sheet music she intended taking with her and put it in her craft bag. 'Shall we go?'

He dug his car keys from the pocket of his jeans and led the way out through the sweet shop.

Sylvia flicked the window display lights on, locked up and got into the car.

The evening was calm and warm, and she sensed excitement in the air. Or maybe she was just affected by being in Laurie's company. She'd never felt so comfortable with a man so quickly and easily. Whatever preconceived opinion she'd had of him from the radio interview had been replaced by getting to know him better. He was easy to like. Too easy to love. She intended keeping her guard up when it came to romance. Laurie was a broken heart in the making. No way she wanted to put herself in jeopardy of that.

He glanced out the window at the loch as they drove by on the way to the castle. 'It's a beautiful loch. So calm and tranquil.'

'And deceivingly deep.' A bit like him, she thought. Were there hidden depths to this handsome man that she'd be surprised to find? Or was Laurie's character what he appeared to be? Too often she'd trusted someone and felt crushed when she'd been duped.

Lights shone from the windows of the cottages sprinkled around the hillside, creating a location that appealed to him. Would he ever consider moving here? He surprised himself by how much the idea captivated him. He glanced at Sylvia sitting beside him as he drove on towards the forest road leading to the castle. Sylvia captivated him more than anything.

An amber sky arched above them, creating a spellbinding scene. The tree–lined road led to the castle's ornate gates that were open wide. Ahead were the gardens, and the castle itself, aglow with lights in the windows. The turrets rose high into the sky, and the windows of one turret, Gaven's private accommodation, shone with lights.

Sylvia's car was parked out front. Laurie parked beside it. They both got out of the car.

Sylvia put her bag on her shoulder and breathed in the early evening air. 'It's another mild, summer night. I can smell the roses and jasmine and whatever other flowers are making that lovely scent.'

'I'll walk you in,' he said.

'It's okay, you don't have to.'

'I insist.'

The front door was open wide and they walked inside together.

Walter was manning the reception desk and smiled at them. 'Good evening you two. I hear there was pandemonium at the sweet shop.'

'The newspaper feature really sparked the sweetie sales,' Sylvia explained.

'The phone's been busy ringing here too,' said Walter. 'Folk want to book a stay at the castle, or find out about the piano bar.'

Chatter filtered through from the function room where Etta, Jessy, Aileen, Penny and other ladies were getting ready for the crafting bee.

Gaven came down the stairs dressed in his smart trousers, shirt and waistcoat.

'The parcel of sheet music arrived,' Gaven said to Sylvia.

'I'm glad. I was wondering if it had been delivered.'

'Sorry, I should've phoned to tell you, but we've been snowed under with interest in the castle due to the newspaper story,' Gaven explained. 'I put the bundle behind the counter.'

Walter reached over and lifted it up. 'Here you go, Sylvia.'

It was quite a large bundle, but she grabbed it willingly, eager to take it through with her to the crafting bee.

'I want to have a look through it to see if there are any song ideas for the opening night,' said Sylvia.

'Then I'll leave the bundle here at the castle when I'm finished.'

'Remember to take the music sheets you left in the piano stool with you,' said Gaven. 'And thanks for all your expertise in organising this collection for the guests to play.'

'This should give them a wide range to pick from,' Sylvia assured him. 'Make a list of the titles and keep it handy so guests can choose what they want to play.'

Gaven valued her advice. 'I'll put a list in the piano stool and keep one at reception.'

Jessy came out of the function room and saw Sylvia standing in reception. 'I thought I heard you. Are you coming through to the bee? We're about to start.'

'Yes.' Sylvia smiled at Laurie, Gaven and Walter and then hurried away to join in the crafting bee.

'Phone me when you intend playing,' Laurie reminded her.

'I will, and thanks again for helping at the sweet shop,' she said, leaving Laurie to talk to Gaven and Walter.

'I hear you're wangling for a new career,' Gaven joked with Laurie.

Laurie laughed. 'It's the sweetest job I've ever had.'

'Were you really bagging the sweeties?' Walter said to him.

'I was. I even bagged more than I snaffled,' Laurie replied.

Walter grinned. 'I'd bag one, eat one, bag one, munch two.'

'If you think he's joking, just ask chef why Walter isn't allowed in the kitchen when there are chocolate truffles and marzipan fruits on the menu,' Gaven revealed.

'I only did that once at Christmas and once at New Year,' Walter said in his defence.

Their cheery chatter swung around to the subject of the opening of the piano bar.

'Sylvia tells me you're taking photos of her playing at the opening evening,' said Laurie.

'That's true,' Gaven confirmed. 'I want to promote the new piano bar on the castle's website.'

'I don't want to interfere, but have you considered filming Sylvia playing the piano?' Laurie suggested. 'The photos won't capture the full effect. They'll look nice on the website, but when it comes to music, people love to actually hear the songs.'

Gaven nodded with enthusiasm. 'You're right. I'll check with Sylvia if she's okay with being filmed. I have someone that makes the wedding reception videos at the castle, though I know he's booked solid at the moment. But one of the local lads, Gare, is handy with a video camera.' He looked at Walter. 'Do you have Gare's number listed?'

Walter checked their contact list. 'Yes, here it is.'

'I'll give him a quick call,' said Gaven. 'Gare is one of the local farmers. He's Fyn's brother. Fyn owns the flower shop in the main street.'

'I saw the flower shop today when I was down there,' Laurie remarked, thinking that if he ever wanted to give Sylvia a bouquet of flowers he knew where to go.

138

The laird called Gare. 'Hello, it's Gaven...'

As Gaven chatted to Gare, and Walter had to attend to guests, Laurie headed outside to his car. He drove to the cabin and went inside. Jumping in the shower, he freshened up, put on a clean shirt and then relaxed by playing his keyboard.

Back at the castle, the ladies were enjoying their crafting bee. Tables and chairs were set up along with the sewing machines, currently occupied by three members working on their quilting.

The nights usually began with the members showing each other what they were working on and catching up on the latest gossip.

Laurie helping out at the sweet shop was a hot topic.

'He stayed to have dinner with me,' Sylvia told them while working on her needle felt robin. 'I'd left my car here at the castle, and he offered to drive me back, so it made sense to have dinner first.'

'Can he cook?' one of the ladies who was crocheting said to Sylvia.

'He stirred the sauce while I cooked the pasta. I kept feeling like I needed to pinch myself seeing him in my kitchen.'

The ladies smiled at Sylvia.

'I think things are certainly hotting up between you and Laurie,' Aileen remarked while hand stitching the binding on her quilt.

'He wore one of the new aprons you made,' Muira told Aileen.

Aileen's eyes widened. 'Laurie wore a sweetie print apron? I can't imagine that, but he must've looked a treat.'

Sylvia showed Aileen the photo he'd taken of the four of them all together.

Aileen and several other members peered at the picture.

'Laurie looks like some sort of chef,' Aileen assessed.

'He does, doesn't he,' Sylvia agreed.

'I brought the other two aprons with me.' Aileen had them folded in her bag and gave them to Sylvia.

'You've made a lovely job of them,' said Sylvia.

The ladies interest perked up when they saw the sweet print fabric, and a few of them wanted to buy it to make quilted items.

'I brought the fabric for your quilt too.' Aileen had carefully folded the fabric and secured it with ribbon and tucked the pattern in with it. 'That's the pattern for the quilt. And there's the extra fabric you wanted,' she added to Muira.

Muira smiled. 'It's such a pretty print and adaptable for various things.'

Penny mended the vintage denim jacket she'd brought to the bee with embroidery thread, making the mending part of the design. 'I'd like to order a couple of fat quarters of the sweetie fabric. It will be ideal for making patches on worn garments.'

Aileen made a note of the orders. And she'd brought sample pieces of the sweet fabric to share with the bee members.

'Oh, this is so pretty,' said Penny. 'I'm going to sew a sweetie patch on to this jacket.'

Other members were happy to accept the fabric samples too.

The crafts the ladies had brought to the bee included quilting, knitting, crochet, embroidery, needle felting and dressmaking. They were all happy to share tips with each other.

Muira was making a little felt owl, and showing Sylvia how to improve her needle felting, when Gaven came through to talk to them.

'Sorry to interrupt, ladies.' He spoke to Sylvia. 'Would it be okay if in addition to the photos of you playing the piano at the opening night, I had a video made too?'

'Yes,' Sylvia agreed. 'Will you film it yourself?'

'I could, but Gare would make a better job of it. I've just spoken to him on the phone and he's on his way up from the farm to have a look at the lighting in the piano bar.'

Sylvia knew Gare. She'd danced with him at the castle's party nights and she liked him. 'I'm going to be rehearsing the songs tonight, so he can film snippets of those to test the sound and the lighting.'

'Fyn told me that Gare's taken a real interest in filming since he got the new video camera,' said Aileen.

'It's a fine camera,' Gaven agreed. 'And it would be handy if Gare could video bits and pieces for the website.' He then glanced at Etta. She was knitting at speed, working on finishing Mullcairn's jumper. 'Okay, I'll let you get on with your crafting.' He jokingly shielded his eyes as he peered at Etta. 'Especially you, Etta. Sparks are flying off those knitting needles of yours tonight.'

'It's a rush job for Mullcairn,' Etta explained without slowing down. 'I want to get his parcel away tomorrow. His Fair Isle jumper with a matching woolly hat and scarf.'

'I'm sure he'll appreciate it,' said Gaven. 'Ah, here's your tea, scones and cakes,' Gaven announced as Jessy wheeled through a silver trolley laden with their usual crafting night treats.

'Chef is spoiling us tonight,' Jessy announced. 'Chocolate cake and chocolate scones.'

The ladies put their crafting aside and got ready to enjoy their tea.

'I thought those were treacle scones,' said Muira.

'Nope, they're chef's new recipe chocolate scones.' Jessy helped serve up their tea.

Gaven headed back through to reception.

Later, while they were having their tea break and chatting, Gare arrived with Gaven.

'I don't want to cut short your tea, Sylvia,' said Gaven. 'But could you let Gare hear you play the piano?'

Sylvia had more or less finished her tea and chocolate scone. She stood up. 'Yes, I was going to practise soon anyway.' She smiled at the ladies. 'I'll see you later.'

They knew she'd planned to practise and continued to enjoy their crafting bee while Sylvia went through to the piano bar. She quickly sent a message to Laurie telling him she was due to play.

Gaven was needed again at reception, so Sylvia walked through to the piano bar with the tall, strapping farmer. Gare was around the same age as Sylvia. He had blond hair and blue eyes, and wore a cream linen shirt and jeans.

The chandeliers and table lights had been switched on, and the Art Deco bar was spotlit.

The doors had been closed and a notice pinned up.

New Piano Bar opening.

Castle guests are invited to attend tomorrow evening.

Cocktails and canapés being served.

The baby grand piano will be played by Sylvia.

Please dress in evening wear.

The notice ensured Sylvia had privacy to practise playing without guests wandering in. She closed the doors behind them.

Gare looked around. 'The laird said this is how the lighting will be for the opening night.'

'Yes, he wants to create a relaxing atmosphere.'

Sylvia had brought her bag and the bundle of sheet music through with her. From her bag she selected a sonata, set it up and sat down at the piano.

Gare had his video camera with him and viewed the room through the lens. 'That's a fantastic piano. I didn't know you played until we heard it mentioned on the radio.'

'You heard the radio show?'

'Yes, Fyn phoned to tell me to tune in. And now you're all over the newspaper too.'

Gare moved close to view her sitting at the piano. 'Could you pretend to play so I can see if the lighting is okay.'

She did as he suggested.

'What song are you going to play?'

'A sonata. I'm rehearsing several pieces tonight.'

They were chatting happily and getting ready to make a test video when Laurie arrived. So engrossed in what they were doing, they didn't notice Laurie walk in until he spoke.

'Am I interrupting?' Laurie's voice cut into their chatter.

Sylvia glanced round at him while she sat at the piano. 'No, Gare's just setting up the video camera. Gaven suggested we video the opening night.'

Laurie eyed the tall, blond–haired man seemingly chatting up Sylvia. Their easy friendship was easily misinterpreted. But Gare did have a bit of a crush on Sylvia. Though there was nothing but friendship with him on her mind.

'I suggested it to Gaven,' said Laurie.

Sylvia blinked. 'Oh, well it's a great idea.'

Laurie smiled tightly. He disliked the sense of rivalry he felt when he saw Gare so close to Sylvia.

'You're the singer, aren't you?' Gare said to him.

Laurie nodded.

Sylvia picked up on the tension between Laurie and Gare. 'Okay, I'll play the sonata.'

She began, filling the room with a soft but stirring resonance that built quickly and demonstrated her playing ability.

Gare held the camera steady, focussed on her, and then moved around slowly to film her from the opposite side of the piano.

Laurie felt his feelings stir listening to her play, causing his heart to beat stronger in time with the music, in tune with Sylvia.

Hearing her play the classical piece on the baby grand touched Laurie in ways he hadn't anticipated. So different from when she'd played the keyboard in the cabin. He knew he couldn't match her playing on such a grand scale, but it made him want to up his game. The snatched moments he'd heard and seen her play were nothing in comparison to this full performance.

As she finished, the notes lingered in the air for a moment.

Laurie applauded and walked over to her while Gare turned the camera off.

The two men matched each other in height, though Gare bore more muscular bulk.

'That was outstanding,' Laurie told her, causing her to smile up at him.

'I think I'll include it in the play list for the opening,' she said.

Laurie nodded firmly. 'You should. It's beautiful.'

Sylvia realised she'd left some of the sheet music she'd brought with her through at the crafting bee. 'I'll be back in a minute,' she said and hurried away to the function room leaving Laurie and Gare alone.

'None of us knew Sylvia could play the piano,' Gare said, filling the silence between them. 'She's always been full of surprises.'

'She's very talented.'

'Sylvia's beautiful too. And a lovely person.'

Laurie picked up from Gare's tone that he was hinting at something.

'She is,' Laurie agreed. 'Have you been friends with her long?'

'We've danced at the castle functions.' He shrugged awkwardly. 'But she's made it clear that she's not yet ready for romance.'

'Did you ask her out?'

'No, apparently, she had a bad break up with an ex–boyfriend in Edinburgh, a rotten apple who did her wrong. So she wants time to settle here in the village before looking for romance again.'

Laurie nodded that he understood. But his heart ached as he realised that any thoughts he had about Sylvia needed to be kept to himself. She'd made it clear that she wasn't prepared to get involved romantically. He valued her friendship, but he needed to realise that romance wasn't on the cards. Not yet anyway. And maybe by the time she was willing to open her heart again, he'd be long gone.

CHAPTER ELEVEN

Sylvia packed her needle felt robin and quilting fabric in her craft bag, cutting short her bee night. 'I'm going to practise playing the piano for the opening night,' she explained, picking up the extra sheet music.

The ladies understood.

'Don't wait for me when you've finished here,' she told Muira. 'I'll probably stay on until it's quite late.'

Muira smiled and nodded. 'Have you decided the songs you'll play?'

'No, I need to select the right mix so I'll do that this evening,' said Sylvia.

'Is Gare going to make a video of you playing on the opening night?' Jessy said to her.

'Yes, he says the lighting and everything is ideal. He's through there just now talking to Laurie,' Sylvia explained.

Jessy frowned. 'Laurie's in the piano bar?'

'I promised I'd let him hear me play this evening.'

Etta's knitting needles continued to spark at speed while she commented, 'There's definitely a romance brewing between the two of you.'

Sylvia tried to suppress a blush. 'Laurie just wants to hear me play. He's heard snippets, but he asked to hear me and I told him it was okay to come over from his cabin and listen while I rehearse.'

'Gare has a wee fancy for you,' Aileen announced. 'I wouldn't leave Laurie and Gare too long in case they start talking about you.'

Sylvia picked up her craft bag. 'There's nothing to talk about.'

'Oh, I think there's plenty,' said Etta.

Sylvia smiled nervously. 'You lot are just stirring things up.'

'Nothing wrong in stirring up a wee bit of romance,' said Etta.

'Plenty of wrong in stirring up trouble,' Sylvia argued lightly.

The ladies giggled.

'Right, I'm away to play the piano. I'll make my wonky robin another time.'

'We want all the details tomorrow,' Muira called after her.

Without looking round, Sylvia waved her hand and continued out of the function room.

Music sounded from the piano bar, and when Sylvia walked in she saw Laurie sitting playing. He'd chosen one of the songs from those that had been delivered. A popular, contemporary song rather than a classical piece.

She walked over and hung her bag on the back of one of the chairs.

Laurie didn't notice her at first, but then he looked up from the keys and saw her standing there listening to him play. He stopped.

'Don't stop,' she told him. 'That sounded great.'

Laurie continued, while Gare filmed the Art Deco bar, making sure he had footage of it. When the bar was busy, he wasn't sure if he'd get a clear shot of it, so although there were no cocktails on display, he had enough of it captured to be part of the promotional video if needed.

'I rummaged through the sheet music you bought and found something that's more in my league of playing skills,' Laurie said to her.

'You should play it at the opening night,' she said. 'People would love it, especially if you performed it. Doesn't the song have lyrics too?'

Laurie nodded and looked at the sheet music he'd set up in front of him. He'd nearly finished playing the song, but sang the final lyrics of the repeated chorus.

Gare glanced round and filmed Laurie's short performance.

Laurie finished on a long, lingering note and added the final flourish of notes to complete the song. He lifted his hands off the keys.

Gare filmed her clapping and then turned the camera off. He could see the obvious spark of attraction between Sylvia and Laurie. Whatever hopes he had of dating her further down the line faded with the music.

'Okay, I think I've got enough to run through at home,' Gare announced. 'I have to get home to the farm. It's a crack of dawn start for me in the morning. I'll see you both tomorrow night.'

'See you then,' Sylvia said as he strode away.

Sylvia sat down beside Laurie on the stool.

Her green eyes flashed at him as she smiled. 'Are you up for a duet?'

No, he wasn't. Even feeling her sitting close to him broke his heart a little. 'How can I resist?'

149

Sylvia looked at the music for a moment and then started to play.

Laurie joined in, and together they replayed the song, doubling up on the resonance, accenting different parts, yet culminating in a performance that was a balanced duet.

Their playing ability sounded well–matched, though Laurie wondered if she played it down while he tried to up his level. Somewhere in the middle, they sounded great together, keeping in time, neither trying to outshine the other.

Gaven walked in and applauded as they played the final notes. 'Perfect harmony. Can I persuade you to perform with Sylvia at the opening?' he said to Laurie.

Not wishing to steal Sylvia's thunder, Laurie glanced at her for a decision.

'Guests would love to hear you play,' she told Laurie.

'Okay, I'll play along with Sylvia,' Laurie agreed.

Gaven smiled. 'I've messaged everyone I know about the opening night. They've all accepted, so it'll be a busy evening, but that's what we want.' He smiled brightly. 'Right, I'll let you two get on with your practising.' He walked out, leaving them alone together.

'Would you like to try another duet?' she suggested. 'In case we need an encore.'

Laurie jolted inwardly. 'I'll try tackling it.'

She got up and went over to where the pile of sheet music was sitting on a table, selected three popular pieces and brought them back for Laurie to choose.

She fanned them out like a pack of cards.

He tried to decide between them. 'What one do you like?'

'This song is lovely and so romantic.' She sounded wistful.

Again, his heart took a hit. Here she was in a romantic frame of mind, and he wanted so much to tell her how he was feeling about her. But he wouldn't, he told himself firmly.

Sylvia frowned, wondering why he was so hesitant. 'If you'd prefer me to find other songs there's a whole load to choose from.'

'No, I was just...' Thinking that I hadn't expected to meet a beautiful woman like you here. 'Thinking that your choice sounds perfect.' The song was familiar, but he'd never performed it.

Sylvia perked up, pleased he agreed, and having her doubts allayed.

She set the music up in front of them.

'Any tips before we start?' he said.

'Play from the heart.'

With Sylvia beside him, this was the only thing he was sure of.

They began, with Sylvia taking the lead and Laurie coming in to join her, adding to the richness of the melody, enhancing the feeling of romance.

'There are lyrics, if you want to sing.'

Encouraged by her, he started to sing as they played.

The words spoke of love and romance, concluding with a happy ever after.

Would his story with Sylvia end so happily he wondered. Or was the romantic duet the closest he'd come to being near to her heart?

When they finished he stood up. 'I'd better collect my new jumpers from Etta. She said she'd bring them with her tonight.'

'Yes, she gave me a peek. She's a beautiful knitter. I think you'll like them.'

He tried to look casual, as if he wasn't stirred to the core. He did want to pop through to get the jumpers, but he needed to quell his feelings for Sylvia.

Leaving her to continue practising, he walked into the heart of the crafting bee.

Etta was the first to smile. 'I've got your jumpers.' She lifted up a bag where they were neatly folded and handed it to him.

He held the first jumper up and admired it. 'This is incredible knitting. And I love the subtle colours.'

'Fair Isle is a favourite of mine,' said Etta.

'Is it okay if I try it on?' he said, not wishing to disrupt their evening.

'Yes, see if it fits,' Etta encouraged him.

He pulled it on over his shirt and stood there for their approval. 'It fits great.'

Etta got up and checked the sleeves were long enough, and that the shoulder seams lay flat where she'd pressed them. 'It does, and it suits you. Try the other one. It's the same size, but an Aran knit pattern.'

Laurie took the first jumper off and put the cream one on. Another great fit. 'I don't know what one I like most. I'm happy I bought the two of them. He kept the second one on and folded the first. As he put it back in the bag he noticed there was a Fair Isle hat and scarf in the bottom of the bag.

He glanced at Etta and then lifted them out. They toned in with both the jumpers, allowing him to mix and match them.

'I couldn't give Mullcairn wee extras and not give them to you too,' Etta explained, pleased to see the delighted reaction on Laurie's face.

He put the hat and scarf on. 'Oh, yes, I'm well kitted out for the colder days.' Then he tucked them in the bag, ruffling his hair after wearing the hat. 'Let me know how much these are and I'll buy them.'

Etta shook her head. 'No, these are just extras for you.'

'Thank you, Etta.' Forgetting himself for a moment, he gave her a warm hug. 'Oh, sorry, I didn't mean to—'

Etta hugged him back. 'I'm happy you like them.'

'We're having another round of tea,' said Jessy, gesturing to the topped up trolley. 'Would you like a cup?'

Laurie sat down at their table. Several tables were set up, and he noted it was a hive of social sewing and crafting. 'A cuppa would be nice. I was singing while playing the piano with Sylvia. I could do with something to drink.'

Jessy poured him a cup. 'Milk and sugar?'

'Just milk, thanks, Jessy,' he said.

'There's cake and chocolate scones going begging,' Muira told him.

'Chocolate scones? I've never had one of those.'

153

'Chef baked them,' said Jessy. 'They're delicious with a slather of butter.'

Allowing himself to be pampered, he let Jessy butter his scone.

'This is really tasty,' he mumbled and then took a sip of tea.

'Are you going to be playing along with Sylvia tomorrow night?' Muira said to him.

'I'd no intention of taking part, but I've somehow agreed to accompany Sylvia for one song, maybe two. Both duets.'

'That'll be something to hear,' Muira exclaimed. 'The two of you playing together.'

'The opening night is turning into quite an event,' Jessy remarked.

Laurie felt a rush of excitement. 'Sylvia playing the classical pieces is what I'm looking forward to.'

The ladies agreed, but added that they were excited about his performance too.

'It was a smart suggestion of yours to have the piano playing filmed,' Etta told him.

'Gare will make a good job of it,' said Jessy.

'I hear he's a farmer. Is the filming a new hobby of his?' Laurie said to her.

Jessy nodded. 'Yes. He's a farmer first and has no intention of doing anything else. But he's taken an interest in filming and it's been handy when Gaven's needed his assistance.'

'Gare's a fine young man,' said Etta.

Laurie ate his scone.

'We're fortunate to have a few men like him in our community,' Aileen added.

'People come and go,' said Etta. 'But there are times when there's a feeling of romance in the community. A few couples have fallen in love here recently. We'll probably see others falling too.'

The ladies exchanged knowing glances, but Laurie focussed on finishing his scone and tea. 'What are you all working on?' He noticed the sewing machines were occupied with ladies stitching quilts.

'Quilting,' said Aileen. 'So are a few others.'

'I'm obviously knitting this jumper for Mullcairn.' Etta held up her knitting.

Penny showed him the denim jacket. 'I've stitched a patch on this vintage jacket using a piece of the sweet fabric Aileen gave me.'

He recognised the fabric. 'That's what the aprons in the sweet shop were made from.'

'That's right,' Aileen confirmed. 'We often share bits and pieces at the bee nights.'

'I've been needle felting an owl.' Muira held it up. 'Sylvia was working on a robin.'

'I'm not sure what needle felting is,' said Laurie.

Muira and the ladies were keen to show him what they were working on, and he was genuinely interested.

'How long have you had the crafting bee?' he said to them.

'A long while now,' Jessy replied. 'Etta used to hold it in her cottage, as did a few of us, and then the laird offered us the use of the function room at the castle. He's always backed the local community.'

'Gaven's certainly made a success of building the cabins to add to the castle's guest facilities,' Etta remarked. 'It's brought people like yourself to the village.'

'The cabin is sheer luxury, and everyone has made me feel so welcome,' he said.

'Would you like a top up of tea?' Jessy offered.

Laurie held up his cup and she poured him a second cup.

'How long are you staying?' Muira said to him.

'A month, but Gaven says I can extend my stay if I want,' Laurie explained.

'Will you be able to stay longer?' Muira wanted to know. 'Or will you have to go home to Edinburgh because of your career?'

'I'm not sure yet. I planned to write two or three songs here and then go back to the city. I record all my albums there.' Laurie took a sip of his tea and looked pensive. 'But the castle and the cabin are so different than I'd imagined. The pictures and information on the castle's website are accurate, but it doesn't capture what it feels like to live here. It's wonderful.'

'As you know, a few guests have ended up moving here and setting up home,' Etta reminded him. 'Maybe you'll do that too. Folk fall in love with the village. And with those they meet here.'

The muscles in Laurie's firm jaw tightened as he bit back the urge to tell them he liked Sylvia.

Picking up the bag containing his other jumper, hat and scarf, Laurie thanked them for the tea and scone and went back through to the piano bar where Sylvia was still playing.

She looked at him as he walked in wearing the Aran knit jumper. 'I'm sorry,' she said, causing him to

156

jolt as she stopped playing. 'The knitwear model night is next week.'

He shook his head at her and gave her a scolding smile.

She commenced playing. 'Etta's made a fine job of your jumper.'

Laurie dug into the bag, pulled out the woolly hat and scarf, and put them on. 'Etta gifted me these extras. What do you think?'

'Definitely knitwear model potential. The hat shows off your chiselled jaw and handsome features.' The second the words were out of her mouth, she wished she could retract them.

Laurie grinned. 'You think I'm handsome?' he teased.

She focussed on her playing. 'You know fine you're a looker. But you're a scunner and a scoundrel, so that balances it out.'

'I'm still lingering on the compliment. Though I'm interested to know why I'm a scunner. Scoundrel...okay, I can accept that.' Pretending to throw her in the pool accounted for that.

She sighed resignedly. 'You were a scunner at first on the radio, and the first time you walked in here and saw me giggling with Gaven, but I suppose that's in the past.'

'It is,' he assured her. 'Though no promises in the scoundrel category.'

'I feel duly warned.'

He took the knitwear off, folded the items and put them back in the bag.

'Want to run through the duets again?' he said.

'Yes, let's do that, especially as you're going to be singing along.'

Laurie sat down beside her and ran his fingers through his hair that was sticking up having worn the woolly hat.

Instinctively, Sylvia reached over and gently brushed stray strands that were across his brow. Then she immediately pulled back.

'It's okay, Sylvia. I'm not precious.'

'Neither am I.'

They looked at each other for a moment, and he sensed that maybe she was starting to change her mind about romance. Rather than guess, or overstep, he came right out and asked her.

'I know that you've put romance on hold until you're fully over your ex–boyfriend—'

'No, he's not the reason,' she cut–in. 'I refuse to have my life controlled by someone who's no longer in it.' She looked right at him. 'I'm the reason.'

Laurie listened carefully. She wasn't being short with him, just straightforward. He preferred that.

'I'd been someone's girlfriend for two years, while I was working at the bakery and training in sweet making. Then the split happened at the same time I'd decided to come here to work with my aunt. I just want time to be me.'

'I understand. I don't mean to overstep the mark. I guess I really am a scunner and a scoundrel.'

Sylvia smiled warmly at him. 'That's okay. And maybe I won't need as much time as I thought before taking a chance on romance again.'

He smiled and then focussed on the music. 'Come on, let's play the songs together.' It was much safer territory. Navigating the ways of the heart needed careful planning. He didn't have a map for that. The routes he'd followed in the past had all ended in an abyss of empty promises and love lost along the way.

Sylvia got ready to play the first duet. 'We should rehearse this one a few times as we know for sure that we'll be performing it.'

'No,' he disagreed. 'You can over–rehearse a song until you beat the energy out of it. It'll sound flat if we do that.'

'Okay.'

'I'm confident that we can do this. There's a strong harmony between us.'

Sylvia agreed. 'I think we play to the same rhythm.'

In his heart he believed this too, though whether this would extend to a romance between them, he didn't know.

Their duet filled the room, and although she didn't sing a word, she felt every emotion in the lyrics he sang.

CHAPTER TWELVE

The crafting bee at the castle was drawing to a close. The ladies were packing up their quilting, sewing, knitting and other items and chatting about what they were going to wear to the piano bar opening.

Most of them intended wearing a dress and seemed to have something suitable in their wardrobes.

'What's Sylvia wearing?' Penny said to Muira.

'We've been so busy, I haven't had a chance to ask her.' Muira pondered this as she packed the aprons and new fabric in her bag. 'She'll have to wear something a wee bit special as she's going to be in the spotlight when she's playing the piano.'

'That's what I was thinking.' Penny had a suggestion. 'I bought a bargain bundle of clothes recently. Vintage, retro, all previously worn. In with the jackets, skirts and tea dresses was a 1930s evening dress. Beautiful condition. I barely had to do any repairs to it. One of the thin straps needed sewn to secure it, and I stitched part of the hem. It's a full–length dress. Maybe the hem caught on a heel when it was worn.'

Muira and the ladies paused to hear about the dress.

'What size is it?' Muira said to Penny.

'I tried it on. It fits me, so it'll fit Sylvia.'

Penny took out her phone and showed it listed on her website. 'I cleaned it, as I do with all my pre–loved items before I list them on my website. I've only just put it up for sale.'

Muira gazed at the pale pink satin dress. 'It's a real bargain.'

'I got it for buttons in with the bundle. I like to pass on bargains like this to my customers,' Penny explained.

'It's a gorgeous dress,' Muira exclaimed.

The other ladies agreed.

'This would suit Sylvia with her being slender,' said Etta.

'I love the colour,' Aileen commented. 'Subtle glam.'

Penny's description of the dress said it was alluring. A V–neck décolletage that didn't reveal too much. Shoe string straps. The back dipped into a long V. The design was bias cut. A figure–flattering dress. Vintage. Classic.

'I'll tell Sylvia.' Muira sounded pleased. 'If she likes it, I'll buy it for her.'

'Sylvia is welcome to borrow it,' Penny offered. 'It's pre–loved. One more outing to a cocktail event won't make any difference.'

'Are you sure?' said Muira.

'Yes, that's what I had in mind. It'll suit the Art Deco styling of the bar,' Penny reasoned. 'Sylvia and you have bought clothes from me before. I'm happy for her to wear it to play the piano.'

'A grand dress for a baby grand,' Muira enthused.

'Precisely,' Penny agreed.

The ladies were buzzing with excitement, and a couple of them noticed dresses that were also real bargains and wanted to snap them up. Among the bee, the ladies had an agreement that discounts were offered when they bought anything from each other.

The chatter followed them as the ladies poured out into the reception. The doors to the piano bar were closed, so none of them disturbed Sylvia and Laurie, and headed home after another enjoyable crafting bee night at the castle.

Sylvia continued to play the piano, while Laurie listened to her renditions of classical pieces.

She finally stopped and wrote down the final song on the list she'd selected. 'I think I've played enough.' She folded the list and put it in her bag. 'I'm up early in the morning to make sweets for the shop, so I'd better head back and get some sleep.'

Laurie watched as she closed the lid on the piano and collected her things.

'I'll walk you to your car,' he said, picking up the bag of knitwear to take with him.

They headed through reception, and Sylvia handed Walter the bundle of sheet music to keep safe behind the desk, before they stepped out into the mild night.

Sylvia breathed in the fresh air. 'I'd forgotten how much I used to love playing. I should feel tired, but instead I'm buzzing with excitement. Probably anticipating the opening tomorrow night.'

'I enjoyed hearing you play. But I didn't expect to be joining you in a duet.'

'You seem to have really taken to the baby grand.'

'It plays like a dream,' he said.

Sylvia unlocked her car. 'Would you like a lift to your cabin?'

'No, it's not far. I'll walk. I don't want to waylay you. You need to get home.'

'Come on,' she said. 'It's on the way.'

'No, it's not.'

Sylvia smiled encouragingly to him, so he got into the passenger seat and she drove off towards the cabin.

A lantern hanging near the doorway glowed in the night, and he'd inadvertently left a lamp on inside.

'It looks cosy and inviting,' she commented. 'Not that I'm angling for an invitation.'

'You're welcome to come inside if you want.'

'Another time perhaps. I'd like to play the keyboard again.'

'We'll get together to play sometime after the opening.'

'Yes, all my focus is on that right now. Plus restocking the sweet shop.'

He got out of the car, but before walking away, he joked with her. 'A subtle reminder. Frying pan.'

'I'll remember to bring a couple with me tomorrow night,' she promised. 'I trust you won't be wearing a kilt, so you won't keep them in your sporran.'

'No kilt. A suit.'

'I've no idea what I'll wear. I'll rummage through my wardrobe and find something.'

'I'm sure you'll look lovely. See you at the party.' He walked towards the cabin.

Sylvia waved to him and drove away.

He stood lit up by the lantern, wishing she could've stayed and played the keyboard with him.

Watching the tail lights of her car disappear into the night, he went inside and got ready for bed.

Sylvia opened the car window and breathed in the night air as she drove away from the castle's estate and down the forest road towards the loch. Nightglow reflected off the calm surface of the water.

She was tempted to stop, get out and meander along the edge of the beautiful loch. Another night perhaps, when she didn't have a full schedule and an early start the next day.

Driving on, she parked outside the sweet shop and went inside, lit by the glow of the display lights.

The tiredness was starting to kick in. The familiar scent of vanilla and chocolate reminded her that she had a busy day ahead, so she didn't linger and headed to bed.

Rewinding the events of the evening, she lay there gazing out the window, hearing the songs in her mind that she'd played on the piano and the duets with Laurie.

The window was open at the side of Laurie's bed and the fragrance of the greenery wafted in. It felt like he was sleeping out in the wilds of the countryside where only the natural sounds of the estate were heard. Nothing else. No one was nearby to disturb the calm. Sheer bliss.

In the quietude, he began to hear a melody start to play, an opening rift at first, and then building to a chorus. He mentally rewound it, deciding it had potential and reached for his phone on the bedside table to record himself humming the tune.

But this wasn't enough to capture the melodic nuances that were layering themselves swiftly in the new song, so he threw the duvet back and, wearing only a pair of shorts, he padded through to the keyboard to start playing and recording the melody.

The song had a strength to it, a depth of feeling that he attempted to capture and convey with every note on the keyboard. He shook himself, wondering if he was overtired, because although he was playing the keyboard, he heard the notes as if he was playing the piano.

Going with the flow, he continued to play, hearing a second verse, and the beginning of lyrics. Singing them aloud, roughly, then repeating them smoothly, he felt he'd come up with a strong contender for the album. If he could finish it.

He believed he could. In the past, inspiration came to him in different ways. No one method outshone the others. Sometimes he'd wake up in the middle of the night with a song in his head, and work on the process of creating it into a playable tune. Many of the songs on his previous albums, and singles, started this way. Others were hard work, and he'd toiled tirelessly to get them to sound right.

But this song... He sensed in his heart that it was a winner.

An evening playing the piano with Sylvia had probably triggered his imagination. She inspired him in ways he hadn't felt in years, if ever.

The dawn was rising by the time he'd finished playing. A pink dawn like the one he'd seen when he'd left Edinburgh behind.

Easing off the tension in his shoulders, but satisfied that he'd captured the essence of the new song, he went back to bed and fell asleep and didn't stir until it was time for the breakfast he'd booked at the castle.

Showered and changed into jeans and a light denim shirt, Laurie walked to the castle, feeling less tired than he'd imagined from the snatched snooze he'd had.

Walter welcomed him. 'Morning, Laurie. Sleep well?'

'I was song writing until the dawn,' Laurie told him.

'You look perky to me.'

'I feel rested. It must the all the fresh air.'

'Tattie scones and a pot of tea are being served at your table while your eggs and hot buttered toast are being made.'

Walter escorted him through to the dining room and seated him at his allocated table.

'I hear you're playing a duet or two with Sylvia tonight.'

Laurie poured himself a cup of tea and buttered a tattie scone, feeling his appetite trigger due to the savoury aroma of the breakfasts being cooked and served.

'I am. Gaven talked me into it.'

'The guests are looking forward to the whole affair. The music, not you and Sylvia. Not that you're having a Highland fling with Sylvia.'

Laurie grinned at Walter.

'I'll zip my geggie and let you enjoy your breakfast.' Walter scuttled away, leaving Laurie smiling to himself as a member of the waiting staff came over to attend to his order.

The vintage dress hung on the outside of Sylvia's wardrobe. Muira had picked it up from Penny's cottage on the way back from the crafting bee at the castle, and brought it with her when she arrived at the shop in the morning.

'I love that dress, and it fits beautifully,' Sylvia said as they worked busily in the sweet shop.

'I'm pleased you like it. I offered to buy it for you, but Penny insisted you could borrow it for the evening.'

'You spoil me rotten.' Sylvia smiled at Muira.

'I'm your aunty, I'm allowed to spoil you.'

They chatted while they packed the online orders and served customers.

'We're still so busy,' said Sylvia, checking the orders that had come in overnight.

'The newspaper story is fair stirring up the trade in the main street. When I was in Bradoch's bakery earlier for our scones, he told me his shop is still hoachin' with customers and he's inundated with orders for his speciality cakes.'

Sylvia scooped a mixture of assorted toffees into bags. 'Things will quieten down again soon. The profits are looking great.'

Muira wrapped up macaroon bars. 'I've ordered in more sweets, the popular ranges, plus sugar, butter, vanilla and other flavourings to make our tablet, fudge and toffee. We'll have plenty of items to keep us well stocked.'

Sylvia was glad that her working day was busy and went in quickly as she was excited about the piano bar opening in the evening.

By six in the evening, she was dressed and ready to go. She wore her hair down, but pinned up at the sides with diamante clasps.

Muira wore a cocktail–length, burgundy dress suitable for the event, and planned to drive them to the castle. Sylvia had told Gaven she'd be there around six–thirty to make sure the piano and everything else was set for the opening at seven.

The loch looked its smooth, calm, beautiful self. On the surface, Sylvia and Muira chatted happily during the drive to the castle. But although Sylvia was never nervous about performing, this whole event stirred her senses and she couldn't remember the last time she'd felt so excited to turn up to perform.

The castle was aglow with lights as they drove up and the front door was open in welcoming.

Muira parked the car.

Sylvia was careful when she stepped out wearing the full–length dress and walked the short distance to the entrance. She carried a bag with some of the music sheets she'd need, and trusted that the remainder were safely stored at reception.

Music filtered out into the night air, sending a shiver of anticipation through Sylvia.

Muira gave her niece's arm a reassuring squeeze. 'You'll be great. I can't wait to hear you playing again.'

Sylvia and Muira headed inside. Usually the reception was reasonably calm, but it was bustling with activity. Gaven, wearing a smart evening suit, was talking to Walter, checking that everything was organised.

Guests were starting to come down from their rooms for the party night, and being shown through to the piano bar.

Gaven looked relieved when he saw Sylvia had arrived. 'Walter, would you show Muira through to the piano bar and make sure she gets a welcoming drink while I chat to Sylvia.'

'Certainly,' Walter said, beaming, and looking smart in his suit too. 'Come on through and I'll organise a whisky cocktail for you.'

Muira smiled at Walter and then said to Sylvia, 'Good luck.' She left with Walter and disappeared into the bustling activity.

'I have the sheet music here.' Gaven lifted the bundle from behind the reception desk. 'I've made a list of all the songs, as you suggested, and I'll have that printed for guests on regular nights at the piano bar. But I thought you would like a copy, just in case things go haywire.'

Sylvia's heart tensed, and for the first time she considered whether there was a chance that her playing schedule could be thrown off kilter. She accepted a copy of the list. 'Thank you, Gaven.'

He carried the bundle of sheet music. 'Let's go through to the piano bar. I've attempted to open the lid of the piano so that I can learn to do this myself. I'd appreciate if you'd check that it's hunky–dory.'

Sylvia walked through reception with the laird, feeling she was already attracting attention. Several smiling faces nodded acknowledgement to her as she walked past them and into the piano bar.

The atmosphere struck her immediately. 'This looks wonderful, Gaven. It feels so classy.' The Art Deco bar was fully lit and the coloured glass of the design and mirror finish made the bar itself a feature.

But the baby grand piano was the king of the castle, polished to perfection, the lid up, keys ready for playing, everything set.

'You've prepared this perfectly,' Sylvia told Gaven, causing him to smile.

'I listened to what you told me, and I checked the information leaflet.' He stood for a moment to admire the piano. 'It's a beauty. It makes me wish I could play it. But I'm not hinting that I want to learn,' he added. 'I'd rather sit and listen to an expert like you playing it the way it was intended. Besides, I've more than enough to do and not enough hours in the day as it is.'

As if to prove this, Walter waved to him from the doorway. 'There's a wee fiasco at reception.'

Again, without any fuss or fluster, Gaven excused himself to deal with whatever needed remedied. 'And may I say, you look beautiful this evening, Sylvia,' he hastened to tell her before hurrying away.

Castle guests mingled with local guests around the bar, some sitting at the tables that were lit with the lamps. She saw Gare in the far corner with his camera, getting ready to film the event, talking to his brother, Fyn, owner of the flower shop. Fyn was a slightly leaner version of Gare, with thick blond hair that he'd tamed and swept back from his handsome face. Both of them wore suits, and acknowledged Sylvia from across the room.

She walked over to the piano, feeling the excitement building. As it faced out towards the room, so did she, but she felt shielded by the sheer bulk of the magnificent piano.

The fabric of her satin dress glowed with an unmistakable glamour that fitted well with the vintage era of the night. It felt comfortable to wear as she sat at the piano and organised the sheet music in the sequence she'd planned.

The opening number was a classical piece that she hoped would set the mood of the evening. Gaven was due at seven o'clock to announce the opening of the bar. Then he would introduce Sylvia and she would play the romantic classic. After another couple of renditions from her, Laurie was scheduled to join her for the first duet.

Glancing around the room, she searched for any sign of Laurie. He hadn't arrived yet. He'd promised he wouldn't be late.

As she went to mildly panic that something had scuppered his plan, Laurie walked into the bar, looking the epitome of classic handsome in an expensive dark suit, white shirt and dark blue silk tie.

Although he probably glanced around the room to take in the splendour of the occasion, he appeared to only have eyes for Sylvia.

His smile lit up her heart as he walked towards her carrying a bouquet of flowers.

'I wanted you to have these as it's a special night,' he said. He'd bought them from Fyn's flower shop earlier in the day. A beautiful bouquet of roses and summer florals, tied with a cream satin bow.

Sylvia stood up, revealing her full–length dress, causing his heart to thunder just looking at her.

'These are beautiful, thank you, Laurie.' She breathed in the scent of the roses.

'And you look even more beautiful,' he said, admiring her. 'Your dress is gorgeous.' And so was Sylvia, he thought, wishing he could hold her in his arms.

'It's a genuine vintage dress from the 1930s. I've borrowed it from Penny. She sells pre–loved clothes on her website and she suggested I wear this as the style is of the era.'

He wanted to say he'd gladly buy the dress for her, thinking it must be expensive.

'Muira wanted to buy it for me. It's a real bargain. But Penny thought it was more practical to borrow it for the evening.'

Her sweetness and natural beauty was twisting his heart in knots.

Walter had been tipped off about the flowers and approached them with a cheery smile. 'Can I take the flowers and put them in water? We've a vase set up ready for them.'

Sylvia was about to hand the bouquet to Walter when Gare came hurrying over. 'Before you take those away, let me film Laurie presenting you with the bouquet beside the piano.'

Seeing Laurie and Walter nod in agreement, Sylvia handed the flowers back to Laurie, and they rewound the moment he presented her with the bouquet so that Gare could film it.

'Got it. Great,' Gare confirmed, and then headed over to the bar where the laird was getting ready to make the opening announcement.

Walter took the flowers away to put them in water.

'I remembered to bring your frying pans,' she said, taking them out of her bag and handing them to Laurie.

He tucked them in his jacket pocket. 'They look tasty, thanks. A treat for later.'

She smiled at him and then glanced around the room.

'Are you nervous?' Laurie said to her. 'I know I am, but you look so calm and relaxed.'

'I'm not nervous about playing, just hoping the evening goes as scheduled. Gaven mentioned that things could go haywire, so that's set me a little on edge,' she admitted.

'Performances usually have moments when things go askew, secretly. I never had any concert or performance that ran perfectly.' He shrugged. 'But with your ability to play, no one will notice. Only us.'

'My experiences are the opposite. So I guess I'll have to improvise and smile if that happens.'

'That's what makes a live performance so exciting,' he said.

'It's starting to get really busy,' Sylvia whispered to Laurie. 'And I think you're being watched. Perhaps there are some fans of your music here and they're eager to hear what you're going to sing.'

Laurie glanced round at the cocktail party audience as guests sat at the tables or stood around sipping the welcoming cocktails that were being served.

Muira stood beside Etta, Aileen and a few of the other ladies from the crafting bee. Oliver, the artist of the paintings that people were admiring, was there too. Penny was accompanied by Neil the goldsmith. Bradoch and other local shop owners had all been invited and had turned up. The familiar faces mixed with those of the castle's guests, creating an audience eager to hear Sylvia and Laurie play. No one encroached on the area close to the piano, and admired the baby grand from where they were.

'People are looking at both of us. Wondering if there's romance in the air. No one can quite figure us out,' he said, feeling that he put himself in the same category. Being with Sylvia felt so right, and yet...romance still felt so far from his grasp.

'If they're looking for romance this evening, they won't be disappointed.' Sylvia sat down at the piano and set up the sheet music for the opening romantic song.

CHAPTER THIRTEEN

A hush fell over the gathering as Gaven declared the piano bar officially open. Guests applauded the laird's brief speech and then he made his introduction to Sylvia.

'Tonight, I have the pleasure of introducing Sylvia, a classically trained pianist, to play for us,' Gaven announced in a sweeping gesture, drawing everyone's attention to her sitting at the piano.

Sylvia smiled, acknowledging their eagerness to hear her play.

A moment's lull...and then she began.

The opening to the piece held their attention, leaving them in no doubt that Sylvia could play the beautiful piano.

Gare filmed as unobtrusively as he could, capturing the full display of Sylvia sitting there playing, and close–ups from various angles including her fingers gliding effortlessly and expertly across the keys.

Laurie sat to the side behind her, waiting to join her in a duet, but kept steady, not wishing to draw attention to himself.

But Gare included him in a few of the frames, ensuring that the popular musician was featured on the video.

Guests had been informed of the filming, and everyone was happy to be included.

The romance of the rhapsody resonated in the room.

Laurie realised that the acoustics reminded him of the sound proofing in the recording studios when he played his music. The castle's substantial walls and structure contained the sounds and the notes resonated throughout the piano bar, clearly touching a few people's hearts.

The music was both emotional and uplifting, but beautifully romantic.

Sylvia glanced at the faces briefly for their reaction while she played, pleased to see that the song was hitting the right notes with them.

Everyone had paused to listen. No cocktails were served at the bar. For the entire song, the gathering listened, enjoying the experience of hearing the classical music that fitted perfectly with the current mood.

Happy that the audience were pleased, Sylvia then went into her own little bubble of playing, remembering how she used to play a baby grand piano. Raising the bar higher than she had at the rehearsals. Surprising even Laurie.

As the final few notes of the song lingered in the air, Sylvia lifted her hands off the keys.

Everyone burst into applause.

Sylvia glanced over at Muira, and they exchanged a nod and smile. Muira was so thrilled that her friends were given a chance to hear her niece play so well. It was one thing to mention that Sylvia could play, and another to actually hear her. The latter outshone the former.

'That was incredible,' Etta whispered to Muira. 'I expected Sylvia could play well, but that was outstanding.'

The other ladies agreed, as did the guests.

Laurie heard how high she'd raised the bar. He stifled the urge to stand up and cheer. He didn't want to hog the limelight or ruin the video, and instead applauded along with the others.

Without letting the atmosphere drop, Sylvia began playing the second piece in her planned repertoire. A well–known sonata.

Hearing the opening bars, a few couples took to the small dance floor and slow–danced to the music. This included Neil and Penny, and Fyn invited Aileen to dance with him. Gaven danced with one of the guests and she beamed the whole time, delighted to be waltzing with the laird.

Two gentlemen, guests at the castle, danced with Muira and Etta. Muira had never danced while Sylvia was playing and this added to the experience of the evening.

Laurie geared up, ready to play the first duet when Sylvia finished the sonata.

Nerves tore through him, but he hoped his outward calm facade fooled everyone. Apparently, it did, including Sylvia.

She smiled round at him as she finished the sonata, and sat to one side of the piano stool.

Gaven announced the duet. 'I'm sure you know Laurie. He's agreed to play a duet with Sylvia. It's a popular song. We hope you enjoy it.'

Laurie acknowledged the smiles and applause as he sat down beside Sylvia.

The guests didn't know what they were going to play, and there was a buzz of anticipation as the two of them got ready to play together.

'Raise your game,' Laurie whispered to Sylvia. 'I'll try to raise mine.' His eyes glanced directly into hers, imploring her to do this.

Her nod was subtle so that only Laurie knew she'd agreed.

They began in unison, each of them raising the bar, creating a duet that took the audience by surprise.

When it was time for Laurie to start singing the lyrics, Sylvia toned down her playing to allow his voice to take the lead.

Another glance from Laurie urged her to keep the level high, and so she swiftly upped her performance. So did Laurie, in both his playing and singing. It wasn't one of his songs. It was a popular number that again caused couples to dance.

Gare filmed all aspects of the duet, and moments when couples were dancing.

Hearing Laurie singing so strong and melodic, and playing with more vigour than they'd rehearsed, made Sylvia understand even more what a great performer he was.

They played so well together that even Sylvia would've been fooled into thinking they'd rehearsed this far longer than they actually had. But he was right, she thought, feeling the energy in the duet.

She could only imagine how well he'd play a song he'd composed. Though she wasn't inwardly angling to accompany him for his own music. Laurie had his own talent by the ton. He didn't need her input. This evening was a one–off to launch the piano bar. But it was a night she'd always remember.

As they finished playing, the crowd cheered and urged them to play again.

Laurie glanced at Sylvia. Duet number two was on the cards.

Without lingering, they began playing the second duet, slipping into the shared rhythm as if they were long–time musical partners.

Laurie's feelings whirred around him. He'd occasionally experienced this feeling when singing and playing a live concert to a large crowd. The energy of such a crowd was palpable and he'd ridden the wave of it, creating musical moments that were rarely replicated with such a sense of magic.

Tonight, he sensed that type of magic in the air, and felt the connection with Sylvia. And he was glad that it was being captured on video. Whatever happened between them. He wanted to have a recording of this to look back on. An evening at the castle, playing duets with a classical pianist on a baby grand. Nights like this were meant to be treasured.

The duet reached a conclusion in perfect harmony. Couples stopped dancing and turned around to applaud. The entire room erupted with the genuine warmth of their enjoyment.

'Phew!' Laurie said under his breath. 'That was incredible and intense.'

'Oh, yes,' she agreed, taking a deep breath, realising she'd been so intent on playing without faltering, especially during the duets. If she made a mistake while playing on her own, fine. But she didn't want to ruin Laurie's duets.

'Sylvia and Laurie are taking a short break, while cocktails and canapés are served,' Gaven announced. 'Then Sylvia will be playing for us again, including a special performance of a classic concerto.'

Catering staff arrived on cue with silver serving trays laden with a tempting selection of savoury and sweet canapés. From tiny tartlets to bite–size smoked salmon and cheese delicacies, to chocolate truffles and rich caramel cups.

The bar staff were kept busy preparing cocktails galore, as Gaven had advertised, with a few special concoctions created for the castle's new venue. Other drinks, some with a classic theme, were available too, along with soft refreshments and tea and coffee.

'Would you like something to eat and drink?' Laurie said to Sylvia.

She looked over at the busy bar, imagining he'd be waylaid if he went to join in the merry melee.

Before she could refuse, Jessy approached them with a tray of canapés and refreshments. She knew Sylvia's tastes and guessed from Laurie's breakfast menus and shopping lists what his preferences were.

An extra chair was beside the one where Laurie had been seated.

'Gaven thought this would save you time and give you a wee break before you play again,' said Jessy. 'Are you both playing again? Or is it just Sylvia performing?'

Laurie hesitated. 'We hadn't rehearsed anything else. The second duo was just a back pocket number.'

'You could play something on your own,' Sylvia suggested. 'What about playing the new single that I heard on the radio?'

Laurie's thoughts were scattered in all directions. This was a great suggestion, but... 'I played keyboards and guitar for that number. It would sound different from the single that's just been released.'

'Most people won't know it yet,' Sylvia reasoned.

Laurie made an instant decision. 'I'll sing and play guitar if you'll accompany me on the piano.'

Sylvia balked at this idea. 'You don't have your guitar.'

'I'll run and get it from the cabin while you play another classical piece,' he said.

Jessy stood there nodding. 'It would be something special if Laurie sang his latest song.'

It would, Sylvia thought, running out of reasons why this was an implausible idea.

'I have the sheet music for the song. I'll bring it with the guitar.' Laurie looked at her. 'Come on, Sylvia. You can do this. You read music like it's a story you're familiar with.'

She felt herself nodding while inwardly she totally disagreed.

Laurie hurried off, winding his way quickly through the guests, leaving Sylvia with Jessy.

'Laurie seems sure you can do this,' Jessy bolstered her.

'I wish I felt the same.'

Jessy nudged her. 'Eat your canapés and get a sip of your soft drink. This will be the cherry on the top of the evening if you can pull this off together.'

Leaving Sylvia to wonder what she'd let herself into, Jessy hurried away too.

Sylvia sat down, shielded by the piano and ate a canapé. She wasn't sure what it was. She didn't even care. Then she sipped her iced lemonade.

Come on, you can do this, she told herself. It's just a completely new song you've heard once and never played before. But if Laurie had the sheet music, she could play it. She'd done it before when learning a new classical piece.

Gazing around at the smiling faces, seeing everyone having such a great time, she decided to relax and go for it. Nights like this were made for creating romance and fun.

Laurie must've ran like blazes to his cabin and back, she thought, because by the time she'd finished her snack, he was winding his way through the guests armed with his acoustic guitar and the sheet music.

'I know you can do this,' he said, sounding confident. 'You picked up the notes easily when you played the keyboard, and you're far more skilled playing the piano.'

She quickly read the music. 'Okay, I'll give it a go.'

Laurie put the strap around his neck, tuned his guitar and got ready to perform. 'I'll nod to you to begin. We'll play the introduction together and then I'll start singing.'

'Where do you come in?'

'Right there.' He indicated the lyrics on the sheet music.

'Fine. If I mess up—'

'Just keep playing,' he cut–in. 'But you won't.'

'I wish I was as confident as you.'

'You don't need to be. I have double the confidence in your ability.' He grinned at her, causing her heart to react to his sexy smile.

Sylvia set up the sheet music in front of her, mentally going over the opening and planning to take it from there. If the introduction sounded smooth, the audience were far more likely not to pick up on any mistakes.

'Jessy told Gaven what we're doing. He's about to make an introduction,' Laurie said to her.

Sylvia glanced over at Gaven and he gave her an encouraging nod.

Here we go, she thought.

'If all else fails,' Laurie whispered urgently, 'I'll grab my guitar and make a bolt for the door while you break into the concerto.'

She tried not to laugh. 'That's your back–up plan?'

'They'll be so relieved to hear you play, that any ripples caused by my interference will be brushed aside.'

Before she could respond, Gaven made the announcement. 'As a special treat this evening, Laurie is going to sing the first single from his forthcoming album. It was played for the first time on the radio recently, but this is Laurie's debut performing it live. Sylvia is accompanying him.' Gaven then gave the nod to Laurie and Sylvia to commence.

'Any tips?' she whispered quickly.

'Play from the heart.' He cast her a smile that warmed her heart, as he gave her the advice she'd given to him.

He stood at the side of the piano and got ready to play. He didn't need to read the sheet music. He knew the song well.

Laurie played the guitar for a few seconds, and then nodded to Sylvia to join in. Within seconds they were playing in harmony, and a wave of excitement swept through the guests who'd stopped to give them their full attention. Hearing Laurie's live debut of his latest song was something special and they wanted to make the most of it.

Gare filmed the whole performance, including the way Laurie glanced lovingly at Sylvia as he sang the upbeat romantic song.

CHAPTER FOURTEEN

Couples took to the small dance floor during Laurie's song, and when it finished they applauded having enjoyed it.

'That was perfect,' Laurie said to her.

'I'm pleased I didn't let you down. I loved playing it.' Her smile lit up her beautiful face, and he fought the urge to kiss her.

'You'd never do that, Sylvia.'

The chatter in the room didn't fade, and it seemed as if they were expecting more music to be played.

'It's over to you now, Sylvia.' Laurie stepped aside and gave her the full spotlight.

At Gaven's instruction, Walter dimmed the lights, creating an intimate atmosphere for the remainder of the evening.

'Are you sure you don't want to play something else?' Sylvia said to Laurie.

'This evening the theme is the piano bar. Play for them,' he encouraged her. 'Maybe I'll play another time.' Maybe not, he thought, but he knew the night belonged to the classic theme of the baby grand.

With the chandeliers dimmed to a soft sparkle, and the main one above her highlighting the piano along with the adjusted spotlight, it created a stage–like ambiance. Intimate. Seductive. Classic yesteryear.

Soft background music filled the gap until Sylvia was ready to play.

Noticing the couples eager to dance together to the songs being played, Sylvia altered her rundown to accommodate the romantic mood.

Instead of another sonata, she played a popular love song for couples to waltz to, followed by a medley of similar tunes she'd kept on hand.

She glanced round at Laurie as she played, seeing the surprised look on his face. Then he realised what she was doing and nodded to her, seeing the dance floor fill with couples.

Playing another two numbers, Sylvia got ready for the final piece. The concerto. Not something couples could dance to, but a fitting conclusion to the opening night of the piano bar.

Another glance behind her to Laurie. He sat sipping a cold drink and put it down to absorb the full atmosphere of the concerto.

After a moment's lull when the last popular dance song was finished, Sylvia caught Gaven's attention and nodded over to him. A signal that she was about to play the concerto to bring the evening to a close.

Gaven thanked everyone for attending the opening. 'Sylvia will now play the final song of the night. A classic concerto.'

Everyone stopped what they were doing and looked over at her sitting at the piano. Pushing the world aside, she created her own little bubble, becoming lost in the playing of the magnificent concerto. Feeling the rush of excitement, remembering the last time she'd played it at a concert to a large audience. It seemed like a lifetime ago, and perhaps it was, because her life had changed so dramatically since then. Happily so, but the concerto still struck a poignant chord in her heart and the feeling seemed to transfer to the audience.

Muira felt her eyes well up hearing Sylvia play. There was something in Sylvia's soulful method that sounded different from other players she'd heard.

Gazing around at the guests, Gaven saw their reaction, everyone forgetting everything else and letting themselves drift solely into the melody.

Laurie knew he'd heard something special that night. He knew too that he was falling deeply in love with Sylvia. If she ever asked him when he knew he'd fallen in love with her, he would tell her it was the night at the castle in the Scottish Highlands, far from the world he'd left temporarily behind.

But maybe he could be persuaded to fall in love with the village the way others had. To move from Edinburgh and make a home for himself here. His decision would depend on Sylvia, and whether his feelings would be reciprocated.

For now, he was happy that he was part of this special evening. A truly wonderful night to treasure.

The crafting bee ladies came over to tell Sylvia how much they'd enjoyed her playing, and Laurie became occupied talking to the guests as Gaven introduced him personally.

The night had been a success, and with the piano bar now officially open, Sylvia put the list of songs and sheet music inside the piano stool for those wanting to play at other evenings.

'Thank you for letting me borrow the dress,' Sylvia told Penny.

Guests came over and asked Sylvia where she got the dress, and this created a buzz of discussion, and reference to Penny's website and other local knitting, quilting and craft websites.

And all the while, Laurie kept glancing over now and then, connecting silently with Sylvia, hoping that their night wasn't over even though the event was drawing to a close.

Gare beckoned to Gaven. 'Is there somewhere private I can edit the video? I brought my laptop with me in case you'd like me to put a makeshift version up so that it's on the website this evening. Later, I can do some fancy edits on it if you want, but I think it would be impressive if it looked like you were able to have the video up the night of the piano bar launch.'

'Yes, come through to the office.' Gaven sounded keen to take Gare up on his offer. 'That would be great. I didn't think you'd be able to do it so quickly.'

They hurried through to the office, nodding at Walter busy manning reception.

'Sylvia didn't falter, so there's no editing necessary for her playing. The same goes for the duets with Laurie. He sang and played well. There's nothing needing cut,' Gare explained. 'The other shots are of the bar, the guests enjoying the music, the cocktails and nibbles, and dancing. The whole night went like a dream. I can do this,' he assured the laird.

'Use my desk. Is there anything you need?'

Gare set up his laptop on the desk and started to transfer the camera footage over so he could edit it.

'No, I'll let you know when I'm done. It'll probably take about half an hour to whiz through it. Then I'll email the finished video to you so you can upload it to your website. Maybe think what caption you want to give it so you're ready to let folk view it later tonight.'

Gaven nodded enthusiastically. 'I'll do that, cheers, Gare.'

Hurrying away to think what he wanted to add, Gaven whispered to Walter what was happening.

'That would be impressive,' Walter agreed.

A few of the crafting bee ladies and other guests lingered in the piano bar, unwinding after the excitement.

Sylvia was due to head home with Muira, and other local guests were starting to leave while those staying at the castle sipped their cocktails knowing they only had to wander upstairs to their rooms.

Couples were dancing to the romantic background music, and Laurie held out his hand to Sylvia.

'Would you dance with me tonight before you go?' he said to her.

'Yes.' She clasped his hand and he led her on to the dance floor.

Taking her in hold, they slow waltzed to the music. Her soft skin and the satin fabric of her dress ignited feelings deep inside him, and he was reluctant to let the evening finish here. But it had to. He knew that. So did Sylvia.

The gentle strength of his arms around her sent sensations soaring through her resolve not to get involved with him romantically.

As the song finished, he let her go. 'I had a wonderful time.'

'So did I.'

Smiling at him, she then headed away with Muira, feeling like she'd left a piece of her heart with him.

Muira dropped Sylvia off at the sweet shop, and as it was only a short drive, they'd barely had time to chat about everything that had happened.

'I'll see you for a proper natter in the morning,' Muira said as Sylvia got out of the car.

'Yes, there's so much to talk about.' Sylvia waved as Muira drove off, and then went inside and got ready for bed.

The satin dress hung on the outside of the wardrobe. In the nightglow shining through her bedroom window, the fabric shimmered beautifully. But she intended giving back the borrowed dress. She'd worn it well, and now it was time for someone else to benefit from the pre–loved vintage design.

Laurie lay in bed with the window open wide. The scent of the greenery was particularly strong, indicating rain was due. As he rewound the evening with Sylvia, her playing, dancing with her...the patter of rain started to hit off the leaves and flowers outside.

He lay there breathing in the scent and listening to the beat of the rain.

The rhythm started to sound like percussion instruments, especially drums.

Nature's music created a melody in his mind, hearing the beat, the rhythm, building into the basis of a song.

'Here we go again,' he muttered, throwing the covers back and getting out of bed. Wandering through to the living room, stripped down to a pair of shorts, he started playing and recording the song on the keyboard. He played for over an hour, but it was still the depths of the night, so he headed back to bed.

But a message came through on his phone before he had a chance to settle down. A message from his manager in Edinburgh.

'Laurie. Call me. It's urgent!'

He called him. 'What's wrong?'

'You're in the news headlines,' his manager told him bluntly. They got along well, and he'd managed Laurie's career for several years.

'What am I supposed to have done this time?' Laurie sounded used to being mentioned in the gossip columns.

'Apparently, you're dating a concert pianist.'

'Sylvia?'

'Yes. I'll send you links to the news articles. The story made one of the print newspapers' deadlines and it'll be out in the morning. But you're already up on a couple of main newspaper online editions.'

Laurie checked the links, and his heart jarred when he read the slanted news. 'I'm not dating Sylvia.' Not yet anyway.

'According to the stories, and the video on the castle's website, the two of you were getting cosy at the opening of the new piano bar,' his manager summarised.

'We were playing as guests of the laird.'

'Sylvia was accompanying you on a grand piano when you played your guitar and sang your new single. You can take this any way you want, Laurie, but my phone's been buzzing with calls asking for details about *Secret Sylvia*. How long have you been dating? Is she one of the session musicians on your new album? Are you aiming for a classic theme for your new songs? You get my drift.'

He did.

'It's gossip, but based on truth, as I've just watched the two of you playing on the video.'

'I didn't realise the video was up already on the castle's website.'

'Well, it is. And you and Sylvia from the sweet shop are apparently making plenty of sweet music together.'

Laurie ran a frustrated hand through his hair, pushing it back from his troubled brow. 'I can handle the limelight, but Sylvia isn't interested in being involved in our business.'

'I promised I'd let you get on with your creative break at the castle,' his manager said. 'But when I saw this, I had to call you.'

'You did right to phone. It's late, but I'm going to call Sylvia and warn her about the storm of publicity that's heading her way next.'

'Next?'

'Yes, the interview on the Mullcairn show caused ripples of publicity in the local press here at the village.' He explained the details.

'That's small time compared with these headlines,' his manager said.

'I know. Maybe it'll all blow over,' Laurie said, trying and failing to convince himself.

'We both know that's not how this will unfold. You're going to have to give Sylvia the short course on how to deal with this type of gossip. She plays beautifully. She looks beautiful too, so if you've fallen for sweet Sylvia I can totally understand.'

'I do like her.'

'Then phone her. Wise her up. Storms like this do blow over, but they can leave a mess if they're not handled swiftly.'

'Okay, I'll call you in the morning, and we'll coordinate things from there.'

Before he hung up, his manager added, 'It wouldn't be a bad idea to have a classical pianist play on your new album. Mix things up a little bit. Give the remaining two or three songs you need for the album a classic vibe. Sexy. Sensational. Smoochy.'

'Smoochy?' Laurie laughed.

'It's late, give me a break,' his manager retorted.

'And getting later by the minute. I'm going to phone Sylvia. Speak to you in the morning.'

Sylvia was drifting off to sleep when her phone buzzed on her bedside table. Sleepy headed, she fumbled to grab it and squinted to see the caller. *Laurie*. She checked the time. What was so urgent at this late hour?

'Sylvia,' he said when she picked up. 'Sorry to wake you.'

'I wasn't asleep.' She sounded half awake.

The lean muscles in his stomach knotted, knowing what he was about to tell her would wake her up with a jolt.

'My manager in Edinburgh just called me. I'm headline news — and so are you.'

Sylvia woke up with a start. 'Why am I headline news? And why are you?'

'The press have seen the video on the castle's website. Gaven must've had it put up quickly to promote the piano bar. He hasn't done anything wrong, and the press would've got wind of it in the morning anyway.'

Through the tiredness, she tried to see the downside of this. 'But that was the whole idea, to promote the piano bar in the castle. I agreed to play and to be in the video. So did you.'

'Yes, and that's all fine. It's just that...they've hinted that you're my new girlfriend. Or secret girlfriend, depending on what outlet we're talking about.'

Sylvia jolted. 'They think I'm your girlfriend just because we were playing duets together?'

'Sort of, but not quite.'

'Explain.'

'From what I've read, they're guessing from the *sizzling hot attraction* between us. Their words, not mine.'

She guffawed. 'Seriously?'

'I'm afraid so.'

'They've just made that up to create a story.'

Laurie was reluctant to agree.

194

His silence filtered through to her. The pieces of the publicity puzzle fitted together in her mind. They weren't wrong. There was an attraction between them. Everyone close to them could see it, sense it. Now it was being emblazoned across the entertainment news.

'What should we do?' she said urgently. 'You're experienced in this. I'm not.'

'We have three options. Two are easy. The third will fry your mind.'

'Let me hear the third,' she insisted, steeling herself for whatever it was.

'We don't deny any of it.'

'What?' Her voice rose several octaves.

'The more you deny something, the more fuel you add to the flames.'

'In a horrible way, that makes total sense. I must be needing some sleep, because I'm going to agree to do this.'

'Once the dust settles, and it will, we can get on with our quiet lives.'

'It hasn't really been quiet though, has it, Laurie?'

He felt inclined to laugh. 'No.'

'Your world is hectic crazy, you know that, don't you?'

'I do,' he conceded. 'But it has its benefits. People need to know about me and my music if I've to have a successful career. It comes with the territory.'

'I accept that. My world is a sweet shop and the crafting bee.'

'And quickly expanding into playing the piano on my new album.'

Sylvia was silent. Had she heard right?

195

'You heard right,' he said.

'You want me to play as one of the session musicians on your album?'

He hesitated. 'Yes, but sort of more than that. I'd like you to help me give a modern, classical sound to the new songs. I've recorded most of the album. But as you know, I'm here for fresh inspiration for the last few numbers.' He glanced out the window, distracted. 'It's stopped raining,' he murmured.

'Is it raining?' She looked out the window. 'I don't see the rain.'

'It was a brief shower, but it's stopped now. I was lying in bed listening to it, and a melody came to mind. I've been playing it on the keyboard for the past hour.'

'Do you usually find inspiration in the wee small hours?'

'No, I think it's being here at the cabin, in the countryside, being with you, hearing you play the piano.'

'Playing on your album, how would that work? Would I need to go to the studio in Edinburgh?'

'Yes, soundproof studio conditions are required. I'd arrange for a baby grand to be made available. You'd probably only be away for a day or two in the city.'

'I'm not sure I want to step into your world.'

'Your playing deserves to be heard, and I could really use your talent on the new songs. I want something fresh on the album along with sure–fire favourites. The rain tonight sounded like percussion instruments. The whole theme of the album could

196

benefit from your classical playing. And the money is great. You'll be well paid.'

'I'm not looking to fleece you for money,' she clarified.

'I know that. I'm just saying that if you're part of the album, you'll receive payment for its success.'

'One or two days playing the piano in the studio in Edinburgh,' she said thoughtfully.

'Yes. You've just spent an evening playing at the piano bar, and I'm pretty sure you'd enjoy playing in the studio.'

Come on, she urged herself. Say yes. 'Okay, I'll do it. But we need to be careful not to lie to people in the village about us being...'

'In love?'

Hearing him say this sent shivers of excitement through her.

'I don't want to give Muira or the other ladies at the crafting bee the wrong impression.'

'I think they have the impression already that...well, there's a spark between us.'

Sylvia didn't argue. 'We get along, I don't deny that. But I'm not ready to get involved, especially as you'll be leaving here and going home to Edinburgh.'

'I understand, Sylvia.' He checked the time. 'It's extremely late. I'm going to let you get to sleep.'

'Goodnight, Laurie,' she murmured.

'Goodnight, Sylvia.'

They ended the call.

Sylvia lay in bed, mulling over the implications presented to her. Somehow, tiredness overtook her figuring out what to do, and she fell sound asleep.

Laurie stood gazing out the window. What a sweet mess he was in. But if he could hit the right note with Sylvia, her piano playing could receive the praise it deserved.

The remnants of the rain glistened on the leaves outside the window, but the thirsty ground drank up the residue. By the morning, no one except those still up in the middle of the night would even know it had rained.

But everyone would know how he felt about Sylvia. He looked at the images on one of the news features his manager had linked to. There was no denying his strong feelings for her. It showed on his face, the way he smiled at her. What did he see when she looked at him? Was he kidding himself that she was the mirror image of him? Did Sylvia have feelings for him beyond some sort of sizzling attraction?

Unable to figure out all the answers, he went to bed and forced himself to try to get some sleep.

CHAPTER FIFTEEN

Sylvia always thought that one of the great things about working in the sweet shop, apart from making the sweets, was being able to chat all day to Muira. They were a pair of chatterboxes, so their morning had circled around the press stories.

Bagging bon bons and mixing marzipan, they discussed another news story that had popped up in the press. The article was a rejigged version of the others, highlighting the looks of love exchanged between Sylvia and Laurie. It was on the shop's computer screen. They'd read the editorial which was minimal and mainly captions to accompany the plethora of pictures taken from the castle's website and video.

Fyn stepped into the shop. 'Gare says it wasn't our family's farm that Laurie wanted Julia to rough it in the barn.'

'Och! Don't fuss about that,' said Muira. 'The papers have wangled a comment from Laurie's ex–girlfriend. It's nonsense. Walter was just putting Julia off the idea of coming to the castle.'

Looking reassured, Fyn smiled. 'Okay, I'll tell Gare.' He hurried away back to his flower shop.

Sylvia and Muira continued their conversation.

'You have to admit that there is a sizzle between you and Laurie.' Muira concentrated on weighing a bag of sweets.

Sylvia's first reaction was to deny it, but then she blurted out the truth. 'Last night, when we were playing the piano together, there were moments when I thought he wanted to kiss me.'

'I'm sure he did. He's awfy taken with you.'

Sylvia wrapped the chocolate frogs that she'd made by pouring a blend of milk chocolate into the frog–shaped moulds.

'I can't say I would've resisted kissing him, just to see if there is a true spark between us.' Then she gestured to the screen. 'But look at the furore in the press. I don't fancy living in the limelight.'

'You fancy Laurie though.'

Sylvia didn't deny it. 'Obviously, he's a looker, and great company.' She sighed wearily. 'I just need time to get to know him better. Though I feel the getting to know each other part has been compressed like a concertina. I feel I know him better already than my ex. Laurie is uncomplicated. His life as a well–known singer is the twisty bit.'

As they were chatting, Penny came in. 'I'll take a bag of your strawberry creams and throw in a few chocolate peppermints.'

Muira dealt with Penny's order.

'But what I really came in to say is, hang on to the vintage dress, Sylvia. Reading the stories in the papers, you're going to need it.'

Sylvia stopped what she was doing and looked at Penny. 'What do you mean?'

Penny was happy to tell her. 'You'll need a lovely dress for the video.'

'What video?' said Sylvia.

Muira bagged the sweets and wondered too.

'Laurie's music video. His songs have videos of him singing and playing. Sometimes the other musicians are included. One of the papers said you'll be playing the piano in his new video.'

This was news to Sylvia.

'So keep the dress for the video,' said Penny.

'Thanks, I'll hang on to it for now,' Sylvia told her.

Taking her sweets, Penny smiled and left the shop.

'I'll need to talk to Laurie about the music video,' Sylvia said to Muira. 'Everything is happening so fast.'

Muira checked the orders. 'The orders are picking up too. The publicity is boosting sales again.'

Sylvia pushed her own thoughts about the video aside and gave priority to the shop. 'It's fine. I'm here today. We can handle the extra orders together.'

'I'll put the kettle on for a cuppa.' Muira hurried through to the kitchen.

While Muira made the morning tea, Sylvia busied herself packing the orders. She'd been up early to make enough tablet, fudge, toffee frying pans, chocolate robins and other sweets to keep them going all day.

'What's in the parcel through here?' Muira called from the kitchen.

'Twinkle lights. I ordered them for the garden. I'll put them up later.'

'Can I have a peek?'

'Yes, I opened it to check them. They look like they'll sparkle well at night.'

'Oh, these are lovely,' Muira confirmed. 'There should be a ball of garden twine in the shed. You could use it to tie them up.'

'Thanks, the twine will be useful. I've been meaning to have a proper rummage in the shed.'

'I used to have a couple of old–fashioned lanterns. They should still be there tucked away.'

'I'll have a look for them tonight.'

Muira brought two mugs of tea through. 'Here you go.'

Sylvia picked up a mug and was about to take a sip when a message came through on her phone. 'It's Laurie,' she said to Muira.

How are you handling things this morning, Sylvia?
Keeping busy at the shop.
I'm in the cabin working on the new songs.
Making progress?
Yes, thankfully.
The papers say I'll be in your new music video. True or not?
True. If you agree.
Penny says I should wear the vintage dress.
You should. It's beautiful.
The shop's getting busy.
Okay. We'll speak later.

Sylvia put her phone away and helped Muira serve the customers.

Once they'd gone, all happy with their bags of sweets, Sylvia told Muira about the message.

'Laurie says it's true about the music video.'

'You should do it. You look beautiful and everyone will get a chance to see how beautifully you play the piano too.'

Sylvia smiled at her. 'You're the best cheerleader I could hope for.'

Muira held up two packets of marshmallows, one in each hand and hoisted them up as she cheered. 'Go, Sylvia! Rah–rah!'

Any tension or trepidation Sylvia had felt about getting involved in the video faded in a flash of giggles. 'I suppose it could be fun. And it won't be for a while. He hasn't finished writing the new songs yet.'

'That's right,' Muira assured her. 'He's still working on the new songs. The video is weeks away. So is your trip to the recording studio in Edinburgh. But it's handy to know what you'll be doing with him in the future if you get involved with him now.'

Sylvia nodded thoughtfully.

Etta came scurrying in, all excited. 'Mullcairn loves his new jumper and the hat and scarf I knitted for him. He got my parcel this morning and phoned to thank me personally.'

Sylvia and Muira were delighted for her.

'He says he was busy with work or he'd have come along to the piano bar opening,' Etta told them. 'But he plans to attend one of the castle's ceilidh nights. I've promised him a dance.' Her cheeks were rosy with excitement.

'Mullcairn at the castle,' Sylvia mused. 'That'll be more publicity for the village.'

'Maybe I'll get my picture in the paper dancing with Mullcairn.' Etta giggled at the thought of it. 'Not that I think the press will imagine I'm his girlfriend. Not like you and Laurie.'

They laughed and chatted for a few minutes, and then Etta left them to get on with their work.

Laurie's day was spent in the cabin working on the songs. Lunch was sent over to him from the castle.

Walter brought it over because he wanted a quick word with him. 'There you go.' He sat the tray down on the table in front of Laurie. 'This should keep you going until your dinner. Chef has made you a nice piece of salmon and a medley of fresh vegetables. Those tatties are straight from Gare's field. The laird tries to support the local community.'

'This looks delicious, thank you, Walter.' Laurie looked ready to tuck in.

'When you didn't come over to the castle for breakfast, we wondered if you were fending for yourself using the groceries.'

Laurie smiled tightly and glanced at the two empty foil tins cast aside. 'Does two toffee frying pans count?'

Walter pretended he hadn't understood. 'You made yourself a hearty bowl of porridge topped with fresh creamy milk and raspberries.'

Laurie played along. 'That's what I meant to say.'

They laughed.

Walter smiled knowingly. 'I'm thinking you'll be in a tizzy with all this gossip in the papers about you and Sylvia.'

Laurie told him about his manager phoning the previous night.

'I feel responsible for making sure Sylvia isn't affected by the publicity, but there's little we can do except ride it out. She's agreed to play the piano on my new song recordings up in Edinburgh.'

'So you'll be whisking her away to the city?'

'Not for a while yet, and only for two days at the most.'

'Well, that sounds okay,' said Walter. 'Gaven doesn't know if he's coming or going today. The castle's phone and website has been red hot with interest. Folk are fair impressed by you and Sylvia playing the piano.'

'That's all to the good, isn't it?'

'Oh, yes.'

'But today I'm hiding in my cabin and letting the storm blow by.'

'You're knuckling down to get your songs written in the artistic seclusion of your cabin,' Walter rephrased with a wink.

Laurie smirked. 'My manager should hire you to handle our press releases. You've got a way with words.'

'I see the press wangled a quote from Julia.'

Laurie nodded. 'Julia won't be happy that I have a new girlfriend.'

'Oh, so it's confirmed now? You and Sylvia are a smoochy twosome.'

Laurie guffawed. 'Expect a call from my manager and a change in career, Walter. Tell Gaven he'll need to find a replacement for you at the castle.'

It was Walter's turn to play along. 'Nooo, I'm built into the turrets. I'm here to stay.' Then he rubbed his hands together. 'Right, get your lunch while it's still hot. Fling the dishes aside. Someone will collect them later.'

Laurie went to get up from the table.

'Keep your bahookie seated. I'll see myself out.' And off he went with a cheery wave.

Laurie tucked into the food, and smiled to himself, feeling lighter from the chat.

After finishing his lunch, Laurie started work again on his music, adding lyrics to one of the songs, romantic lyrics that he was sure reflected his feelings for Sylvia.Later, he looked out the window at the mellow amber glow of the sky and decided to go for a walk to ease the tension of the day.

He followed a different route from the one he'd walked with Sylvia, exploring another part of the estate. The summer air was warm, but refreshed his senses after the intensity of the day song writing.

He'd exchanged messages with his manager throughout the day, keeping updated about the publicity in the press. Some of the papers had contacted his manager looking for information about Laurie's new girlfriend, Sylvia, and his forthcoming album. His manager obliged them with details of the latter while side–stepping the former.

Mullcairn wanted Laurie back on his radio show as soon as he had a new song, a new single on release, preferably one involving Sylvia's piano playing, and she was invited on the show along with Laurie.

His manager had tentatively agreed to do this with Mullcairn.

Laurie hadn't heard another peep from Sylvia all day, and he'd decided to give her time to breathe, intending to call her later after dinner.

Circling back to the cabin, Laurie admired the golden hour glow, and another melody, a missing piece of the second song he was working on, started to filter through his mind. He stopped in the quietude to record it on his phone, humming the distinctive notes, hearing how he'd play this for the opening rift on his guitar.

No one heard him. No one disturbed him. It was like being in nature's soundproof studio. The perfect atmosphere for making memorable music.

With the melody safely in his phone, he headed back to the cabin to continue working on the song.

Sylvia and Muira tidied up the sweet shop at the end of the hectic but happy day.

Taking her apron off, Sylvia hung it up, and smoothed down the summery, floral print tea dress she was wearing with a pair of comfy pink pumps.

Muira turned the shop sign to closed and picked up her bag. 'I'm going to relax and get my knitting done this evening and maybe some needle felting. What about you?'

Sylvia glanced out the window. 'It's a gorgeous night. I'll hang the twinkle lights in the garden.'

'Check that the twine is in the shed. If not, I think I've got some at my house if you need it.'

Sylvia ran out to the garden and rummaged quickly through the shed. She found the twine on a shelf. But she found something else. Hidden under a tarpaulin at the back of the shed. She'd assumed it was just garden furniture covered up.

Throwing the protective tarpaulin off it, she wheeled the pretty pink bicycle out of the shed and into the garden.

'Muira,' she called into the shop. 'There's a lovely pink bicycle in the shed!'

'Oh, that's my bicycle. I've been so busy with the shop these past months that I forgot about it. I used to like a wee cycle around the loch.'

'Can I have a go?' Sylvia sounded excited. 'I used to love cycling, but I haven't done it in years.'

'Yes, use it whenever you want. I had new tyres put on it. It's a vintage–style bike. I bought it locally. Check if the tyres need air in them.'

Sylvia checked. 'Maybe a wee bit of air. I know how to do it. I don't want to keep you. Enjoy your knitting.'

'Okay, I'll see you in the morning. Phone me if there's any more pandemonium or publicity.' Muira giggled and headed out of the shop.

Sylvia used the bicycle pump to add air to the tyres, thrilled that there was a bike she could ride around on.

Gazing up at the amber sky and feeling the warmth of the early evening, she decided to take it out and cycle around the loch before making dinner.

There wasn't a breeze as Sylvia set off from the shop. But she found the bicycle a breeze to use, as if it was made for her. A sense of freedom, of mischief, excitement and adventure created a heady mix as she pedalled towards the loch.

Within minutes she was there, viewing the loch from a whole different angle, admiring the fading amber sunlight glinting off the surface of the calm water. Bees were busy in the clover. She couldn't see them, but she could hear the familiar buzz. Butterflies wafted over the wildflowers and greenery that fringed the loch, and the quietude created from the natural insulation of the surrounding rolling hills, melted any tension she'd built up during the hectic day at the sweet shop.

Circling the loch once, it had been her intention to head back to the shop. But it was such a gorgeous summer evening and the sense of freedom and adventure overtook her plans.

With the hem of her dress fluttering around her knees, and the amber sun casting everything in its mellow glow, she headed away from the loch, taking the forest road leading to the castle's estate.

Picking up speed on a part of the road where it was flat, she giggled to herself. All the fuss from the press blew away behind her, and she forged on towards the estate. She'd no intention of going near the castle, or Laurie's cabin. The estate was so vast she didn't need to. There were paths that wound their way into scenic routes through the estate, and she whizzed along, loving the sense of being out and about in the early evening.

The first warning of an approaching rainstorm happened when she emerged from an archway of roses into a clearing. The amber light in the sky had quickly become a burnished bronze, and there was a sudden change in the air. The warmth felt dampened. The scent of the greenery and flowers was potent. A sign of impending rain. The weather in the village was never threatening, but it never bluffed when it came to a downpour. If it looked like it was going to rain. It would rain. Run for shelter, or get drookit.

She kept going, glancing around to find the fastest route back to the forest road, but she wasn't familiar with her surroundings.

She glanced up.

Dark grey clouds were pressing the breath out of the sky.

A distant rumble of thunder.

Then she saw a part of the estate that was familiar. She'd been there with Laurie. She cycled across the little wrought iron bridge over the stream. Following the recognisable route, she headed towards his cabin.

Spits of rain began to hit off her bare arms and legs, stinging mildly, warning her of what was on its way.

Peddling like blazes along the narrow path, she reached a clearing where the wind blew through her hair and her dress. This wasn't just a bit of rain, this was going to be a rainstorm.

She peddled harder, faster, making progress, but then the sky opened up. Unshielded against the torrents that poured down, she was soaked in seconds.

Catching her breath, she forged on.

Under an archway of trees she gained momentary shelter, but the rain was already starting to flood the ground around the roots of the trees. Her bicycle would become bogged down if she stayed there, so she continued on. Surely she wasn't far from Laurie's cabin.

She'd no intention of disturbing him. Just using it as a beacon to then continue on, probably to the castle for shelter. The forest road and the loch could be unreachable in these conditions.

She shook her head, her hair dripping wet. She muttered to herself. 'Of all the nights to find a pretty pink bicycle and go for a relaxing ride around the loch!'

If she'd stuck to her original plan of a lap round the loch, she'd be home and dry, sipping a cup of tea, cosy, gazing out the window watching the rain instead of facing the force of it.

'Jings!' she spluttered. It was getting heavier. And so were the muscles in her thighs. What a workout. Nature's gym was a challenge.

Laurie had made dinner for himself. Seeing the approaching storm, he didn't want the castle's staff traipsing out just to bring him a meal. There was plenty of food in the cabin's kitchen, so he'd whipped up a cheese omelette and a salad with tomatoes and peppers. A chunk of fresh, crusty bread and butter, and he was satisfied and filled.

Sitting at the table drinking tea, he scrolled through properties for sale in the village and surrounding area.

There were a handful that caught his eye and appealed to him. Not that he intended buying something right now, but he wanted to gauge the market. Everything in his bones told him there was a strong chance he'd move here. First and foremost because of Sylvia. And he did love the whole environment. If things went well with Sylvia in the coming weeks, he'd extend his stay at the cabin while he secured a house here in the Scottish Highlands. The city wasn't too far away. Others, like the goldsmith, and the laird himself managed to juggle the two. He could too. Maybe then, the main hurdle preventing Sylvia and him getting together could be overcome.

The rain drummed a resounding beat off the roof of the cabin. Another song beat in the making.

He stepped outside the cabin, sheltered by the overhanging roof, cupping his mug of tea and enjoying the energy of the rainy atmosphere.

From the corner of his eye he saw a bedraggled figure on a pink bicycle peddling like blazes through the rain, but not getting far due to the soggy conditions of the grassy path and puddles.

He blinked and gasped. 'Sylvia?'

She didn't hear him call her name for the sound of the rain.

Dumping his mug on the window sill, he ran towards her, and without hesitation he gathered Sylvia and the bicycle in his strong arms.

'Laurie!'

She didn't even feel the puddles and sludge on the ground as he hoisted her up easily and dashed back to the cabin.

He set her down safely on the cabin's small porch and propped the bike up against the cabin.

'Whatever are you doing?' he said, ushering her inside and closing the door against the rainy night.

Standing there, dripping from head to toe, she looked like a discarded rag doll that someone had cast out into a rain storm. Her flimsy floral dress clung to every curve of her body, hiding little and revealing plenty.

'I found Muira's bicycle in the sweet shop's garden shed. I used to love cycling, and couldn't resist taking it for a spin around the loch. It was such a warm evening. I didn't set out too late, but then I was enjoying myself so much, and I headed up to the estate.' She heard herself babbling.

He nodded, taking in her explanation.

'There was no sign of rain when I set out,' she insisted. 'But downpours occur here without warning.' She held her arms out to the sides of her soaked dress. 'I didn't plan to disturb you. I thought you'd be inside and wouldn't see me. I was using the cabin as a marker to find the right route back down to the loch or the castle.'

'Let's get you dried off.' Gently grasping her shoulders, he turned her around and showed her through to the bedroom. 'Help yourself to dry clothes from my wardrobe.'

Her wide eyes blinked at him. 'I'm sorry for being a nuisance.'

'You're not. But you will be if you don't hurry up and get changed out of those wet clothes.'

Closing the bedroom door to give her privacy, he left her to rummage through his wardrobe.

She opened the doors and saw the expensive and pristine selection of shirts, two suits, silk ties, and balked at the thought of ruining any of them. His black jeans looked like they would swamp her, and he was wearing his other pair of blue jeans along with a denim shirt.

'Take anything you want, Sylvia. Don't fuss about ruining any.'

He'd nailed her reservations, so she dug into the wardrobe, picked a classy white and blue pinstripe shirt that looked longer than the others and laid it on the bed while she peeled her dress off and dropped it on the wooden floor where any drips could be mopped up. Tip–toeing around the scatter rugs, she put the shirt on, rolled up the sleeves until she could see her hands, and belted it with one of his ties.

'Here's a towel.' His hand came round the bedroom door and dangled the clean towel.

'Thanks.' She clasped hold of it, dried her hair, and patted it on other parts of herself.

Opening one of the drawers in his dresser, she helped herself to a pair of his clean socks.

She hadn't even brought her bag with her when she went cycling, and finger dried her hair into a messy, but sexy, makeshift style.

Glancing in the mirror, she wiped a smudge of mascara from under her eyes. She wasn't wearing much makeup, so she looked quite fresh faced from the elements.

Suitably rescued from the rain, she padded through to the living room where Laurie had made her a hot mug of tea. He'd put it down on the table beside the couch.

Seeing her standing there wearing his shirt like a fashion statement dress, his heart thundered louder than the storm.

There was a blanket folded on the couch. 'Sit down and put the blanket around you to get some proper heat in your body.'

Without waiting for her to attempt this herself, he wrapped it around her shoulders.

Towering over her, she felt his strength and kindness. She realised how his caring masculinity made her feel. The attraction was so potent she forced herself to look away and concentrate on getting warm. Though she secretly thought there was enough heat in her body to ignite a bonfire. She sensed he felt the same, seeing the flames of desire flicker in the depths of his eyes.

A moment of truth, she thought. Romance with Laurie would have its richness and rewards, but she was only interested in him, the loving, caring, talented man standing so close to her.

Laurie stepped closer.

She didn't back away.

'Take a chance on us, Sylvia,' he murmured, gazing at her with true love in his heart.

Whatever had caused her to hesitate in the past, she let it go, putting it behind her. She'd never been one to want to live in the past. Learn from it, remember it, certainly, but not be ruled by it.

Laurie's arms wrapped around her. He pulled her close and kissed her.

She reciprocated his love, letting go of the past and looking forward to a future with this wonderful man. The sweetest man she'd ever known.

'I'm falling in love with you, Sylvia,' he murmured.

'I'm falling in love with you, Laurie.'

He kissed her again with passion and promise of happiness together.

Sylvia had heard the well–meaning gossip that there was an obvious attraction between the two of them. There were comments from the start about them making sweet music together, in more ways than one. This time, she agreed. She knew she was in tune with Laurie. They were in loving tune with each other.

End

About the Author:

De-ann Black is a bestselling author, scriptwriter and former newspaper journalist. She has over 100 books published. Romance, thrillers, espionage novels, action adventure. And children's books (non-fiction rocket science books and children's fiction). She became an Amazon All-Star author in 2014 and 2015.

She previously worked as a full-time newspaper journalist for several years. She had her own weekly columns in the press. This included being a motoring correspondent where she got to test drive cars every week for the press for three years.

Before being asked to work for the press, De-ann worked in magazine editorial writing everything from fashion features to social news. She was the marketing editor of a glossy magazine.

She is also a professional artist and illustrator. Embroidery design, fabric design, dressmaking, sewing, knitting and fashion are part of her work.

Additionally, De-ann has always been interested in fitness, and was a fitness and bodybuilding champion, 100 metre runner and mountaineer. As a former N.A.B.B.A. Miss Scotland, she had a weekly fitness show on the radio that ran for over three years.

De-ann trained in Shukokai karate, boxing, kickboxing, Dayan Qigong and Jiu Jitsu. She is currently based in Scotland.

Her 16 colouring books are available in paperback, including her latest Summer Nature Colouring Book and Flower Nature Colouring Book.

Her latest embroidery pattern books include: Floral Garden Embroidery Patterns, Christmas & Winter Embroidery Patterns, Floral Spring Embroidery Patterns and Sea Theme Embroidery Patterns.

Website: Find out more at: www.de-annblack.com

Fabric, Wallpaper & Home Decor Collections:
De-ann's fabric designs and wallpaper collections, and home decor items, including her popular Scottish Garden Thistles patterns, are available from Spoonflower.
www.de-annblack.com/spoonflower

Also by De-ann Black (Romance, Action/Thrillers & Children's books). See her Amazon Author page or website for further details about her books, screenplays, illustrations, art, fabric designs and embroidery patterns.

Amazon Author page:
www.De-annBlack.com/Amazon

218

Romance books:

Snow Bells Haven series:
1. Snow Bells Christmas
2. Snow Bells Wedding
3. Love & Lyrics

Scottish Highlands & Island Romance series:
1. Scottish Island Knitting Bee
2. Scottish Island Fairytale Castle
3. Vintage Dress Shop on the Island
4. Fairytale Christmas on the Island

Scottish Loch Romance series:
1. Sewing & Mending Cottage
2. Scottish Loch Summer Romance
3. Sweet Music

Quilting Bee & Tea Shop series:
1. The Quilting Bee
2. The Tea Shop by the Sea
3. Embroidery Cottage
4. Knitting Shop by the Sea
5. Christmas Weddings

Sewing, Crafts & Quilting series:
1. The Sewing Bee
2. The Sewing Shop
3. Knitting Cottage (Scottish Highland romance)
4. Scottish Highlands Christmas Wedding

The Cure for Love Romance series:
1. The Cure for Love
2. The Cure for Love at Christmas

Cottages, Cakes & Crafts series:
1. The Flower Hunter's Cottage
2. The Sewing Bee by the Sea
3. The Beemaster's Cottage
4. The Chocolatier's Cottage
5. The Bookshop by the Seaside
6. The Dressmaker's Cottage

Scottish Chateau, Colouring & Crafts series:
1. Christmas Cake Chateau
2. Colouring Book Cottage

Summer Sewing Bee

Sewing, Knitting & Baking series:
1. The Tea Shop
2. The Sewing Bee & Afternoon Tea
3. The Christmas Knitting Bee
4. Champagne Chic Lemonade Money
5. The Vintage Sewing & Knitting Bee

Tea Dress Shop series:
1. The Tea Dress Shop At Christmas
2. The Fairytale Tea Dress Shop In Edinburgh
3. The Vintage Tea Dress Shop In Summer

The Tea Shop & Tearoom series:
1. The Christmas Tea Shop & Bakery
2. The Christmas Chocolatier
3. The Chocolate Cake Shop in New York at Christmas
4. The Bakery by the Seaside
5. Shed in the City

Christmas Romance series:
1. Christmas Romance in Paris
2. Christmas Romance in Scotland

Oops! I'm the Paparazzi series:
1. Oops! I'm the Paparazzi
2. Oops! I'm Up To Mischief
3. Oops! I'm the Paparazzi, Again

The Bitch-Proof Suit series:
1. The Bitch-Proof Suit
2. The Bitch-Proof Romance
3. The Bitch-Proof Bride
4. The Bitch-Proof Wedding

Heather Park: Regency Romance
Dublin Girl
Why Are All The Good Guys Total Monsters?
I'm Holding Out For A Vampire Boyfriend

Action/Thriller books:

Knight in Miami
Agency Agenda
Love Him Forever
Someone Worse

Electric Shadows
The Strife Of Riley
Shadows Of Murder
Cast a Dark Shadow

Children's books:

Faeriefied
Secondhand Spooks
Poison-Wynd

Wormhole Wynd
Science Fashion
School For Aliens

Colouring books:

Summer Nature
Flower Nature
Summer Garden
Spring Garden
Autumn Garden
Sea Dream
Festive Christmas
Christmas Garden
Christmas Theme

Flower Bee
Wild Garden
Faerie Garden Spring
Flower Hunter
Stargazer Space
Bee Garden
Scottish Garden
Seasons

Embroidery Design books:

Sea Theme Embroidery Patterns
Floral Garden Embroidery Patterns
Christmas & Winter Embroidery Patterns
Floral Spring Embroidery Patterns
Floral Nature Embroidery Designs
Scottish Garden Embroidery Designs

Printed in Great Britain
by Amazon

48666637R10129